THE JUNIOR NOVEL

UNIVERSAL PICTURES and STUDIOCANAL PRESENT A WORKING TITLE PRODUCTION A JONATHAN FRAKES FILM "THUNDERBIRDS" BILL PAXTON ANTHONY EDWARDS SOPHIA MYLES AND BEN KINGSLEY CASTING BY MARY SELWAY CDG FIONA WEIR MUSIC BY HANS ZIMMER COSTUME DESIGNER MARIT ALLEN EDITOR MARTIN WALSH A.C.E. PRODUCTION DESIGNER JOHN BEARD DIRECTOR OF PHOTOGRAPHY BRENDAN GALVIN EXECUTIVE PRODUCERS DEBRA HAYWARD LIZA CHASIN PRODUCED BY TIM BEVAN ERIC FELLNER MARK HUFFAM STORY BY PETER HEWITT and WILLIAM OSBORNE SCREENPLAY BY WILLIAM OSBORNE and MICHAEL McCULLERS STUDIO CANAL DIRECTED BY JONATHAN FRAKES www.thunderbirdsmovie.com A UNIVERSAL RELEASE UNIVERSAL

Thunderbirds: The Junior Novel

Library of Congress catalog card number: 2003115075

Book design by Rick Farley

1 2 3 4 5 6 7 8 9 10

❖

First Edition
www.harperchildrens.com

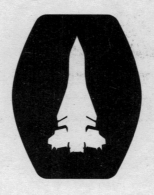

THUNDERBIRDS™
THE JUNIOR NOVEL

Adapted by Stephen D. Sullivan

Based on a motion picture screenplay written
by William Osborne and Michael McCullers

Story by Peter Hewitt and William Osborne

Based on the original television series
"Thunderbirds" © ITC Distribution, LLC

HarperFestival®
A Division of HarperCollinsPublishers

In the year 2010, billionaire ex-astronaut Jeff Tracy lost his wife in a tragic accident. Consumed by grief, he took his five sons to an uncharted island in the Pacific to rebuild their lives.

There he built the secret headquarters of International Rescue—an organization dedicated to helping those in need, wherever and whenever disaster strikes. This group and their incredible machines are both known as . . .

THUNDERBIRDS!

5   **4**   **3**   **2**   **1**

THUNDERBIRD 5: This orbiting space station allows International Rescue to monitor emergencies around the globe. Rescue operations begin here.

THUNDERBIRD 4: A small, powerful submarine, *Thunderbird 4* can penetrate the deepest depths of the ocean. It is often carried to rescue sites by *Thunderbird 2*.

THUNDERBIRD 3: This mighty rocket not only carries the crew to *Thunderbird 5*, it is also invaluable in space rescues.

THUNDERBIRD 2: The workhorse of the Thunderbird fleet, *Thunderbird 2* carries the special equipment International Rescue needs to save lives.

THUNDERBIRD 1: Faster than any jet, *Thunderbird 1* takes the lead in getting help to disaster areas. *Thunderbird 1* is always the first on the scene of a rescue.

Thunderbirds are *go!*

1

What You Don't Know . . .

Alan Tracy leaned over the souped-up motor scooter and brushed his unruly blond hair out of his eyes. He tried hard to look cool and grown-up, but the metal retainer straightening his teeth betrayed him. It was tough being the fourteen-year-old son of a billionaire former astronaut. Even here, in middle of the woods, people looked at you differently. Alan ignored the other boys pointing and whispering nearby. He glanced impatiently at the teenager working on his scooter.

Fermat Hackenbacker had thick glasses, a high forehead, and clothes that never quite matched. He shared these traits with his father, "Brains"

Hackenbacker—the scientific genius behind the Thunderbirds. Fortunately for Alan, Fermat had also inherited his father's inventive brilliance. Fermat could work miracles with machines, and Alan often expected him to.

"A—Alan," Fermat said nervously, "are you sure this is a sm—sm— good idea?"

"Don't worry, Fermat," Alan replied, ignoring his best friend's stutter, as usual. "Just tell me it's going to be fast." Alan swung his leg over the seat of the modified Vespa scooter and focused his eyes on the tree-lined path ahead.

"Less weight, more power," Fermat said. "Yes, it should be quite f—fast."

"Good. Fast is what I want."

Fermat raised an eyebrow at his friend. "Where did you get this propulsion unit anyway?"

Alan smiled. "Fermat, what you don't know can't hurt you. Come on. It's race time."

He pushed the modified Vespa out of the thicket and to the start of the "course." The raceway was really just an old dirt path winding through the woods behind Wharton Academy. For the students, the makeshift track provided welcome relief from the mind-numbing routine of the upstate New York boarding school.

Alan lived for these races; they helped him forget that he was thousands of miles away from home. They also took his mind off the rest of his family, who got to live exciting, heroic lives, while he languished here with students who snickered behind his back. During a race, for just a few moments, Alan felt like a Thunderbird.

The other boys lined up against him all wanted to win the race, too, but none of them had as much on the line as Alan did. Thunderbirds did *not* lose. Alan wasn't about to let anyone or anything stand between him and his dreams.

Fermat continued to make adjustments as Alan rolled the Vespa to the starting line. "All fi—fi—done. I hope you can handle this much power. We've concentrated entirely on p—p—propulsion, without upgrading the guidance system."

Alan kick-started the machine and the oversized motor roared to life. He smiled. "I don't need guidance."

A lookout posted farther down the trail gave the racers the all-clear signal. The racers shot off the line and through the woods. Alan leaned over the handlebars, mentally urging the Vespa forward as he gunned the throttle. The trees on either side whipped by him in a blur of motion.

The other boys zoomed and skidded beside him, having trouble keeping up. Their rugged tires bit into the soil, kicking clods of dirt into the air. Alan leaned hard into the first turn. For a moment, his stomach fluttered. Fermat was right about the steering; it wasn't too good.

Alan could live with it. His family had a history of handling powerful machines. He fought to keep the Vespa under control. The other racers skidded through the turn, having more trouble than Alan had. His lead widened as he shot toward the embankment jump just ahead.

He hit the hill's edge and soared through the air, rising ten feet over the top of the road leading to the school. He landed on the opposite bank and skidded left, barely missing the big sign set atop the slope. WHARTON ACADEMY, it read, with the school's motto below: DUTY. DISCIPLINE. DIGNITY. A clod of dirt flew off Alan's tires and splattered on the sign as he darted into the woods once more.

Alan glanced back as a high-pitched whine filled his ears. Impossible as it seemed, one of the other students had almost caught up to him. It was Ian Welch, a red-headed know-it-all kid from Massachusetts. Alan was always the butt of Ian's jokes.

Alan gritted his teeth. He refused to let Ian beat him this time. He twisted the Vespa's throttle open all the way and surged forward. His hyper-scooter pulled ahead of Ian's and shot away from the rest of the pack. For a moment, elation filled Alan's chest.

Then he hit a bump on the dirt path. The Vespa's handlebars wobbled wildly, and the whole machine began to shake. Alan turned the steering frantically, trying to keep control. He should have listened to Fermat; the power was too much for the guidance system.

Alan missed the next turn and crashed into the brush. He hung onto the Vespa for dear life as trees and bracken flew past. Branches tore at his clothes and scratched his face and bare arms.

He surged out of the forest and rocketed uncontrollably downhill toward the brick school building. Alan tugged hard on the steering, but the scooter refused to respond. He hit another bump and went airborne again, the Vespa nearly flying out from under him. A small pond zoomed toward him. He had no way to avoid it.

Alan and the Vespa splashed down hard, sending up a great geyser of water as they hit. Students and faculty who were gathered near the pond yelped in surprise and rushed away from the scene of the accident—all except a stern-looking, middle-aged man in a tweed suit.

Alan looked up at the man and grinned sheepishly. "Good morning, sir," he said.

The man scowled and wiped the water from the steel-rimmed glasses perched atop his hawkish nose. His wet toupee resembled a drowned rat draped over his balding forehead. The man's new tweed suit looked as though it had just come out of the washer.

A smile of realization slowly tugged up the corners of the man's mouth. Twenty minutes earlier he had discovered the engine missing from his small car. Gazing down at Alan Tracy's hyper-scooter, school headmaster Brian Tierney realized he had found the cause of his "engine trouble."

Knowing Alan Tracy, the principal of Wharton Academy wasn't the least bit surprised.

"W—w—well, how did it go?" Fermat asked nervously.

Alan kept walking, leading his friend down the hall, away from the headmaster's office. "The forecast calls for a suspension, with increasing likelihood of being expelled later in the week," he replied. Seeing Fermat's shocked expression, he added, "Don't worry. It's no big deal." He forced a smile.

"It's a big d—d—deal to me," Fermat said, his voice cracking as it rose in pitch. "I actually *care* about school and grades and all that other stuff you make fun of." He moaned and turned his head toward the oak-paneled wall. "Why do I let you get me into these things?"

"Fermat," Alan said, "I told them you had nothing to do with it. What you don't know can't hurt you—remember?"

Fermat glanced skeptically at his best friend. Alan put his arm around the bespectacled boy's shoulder. "Don't worry," Alan said, trying hard to feel as confident as he sounded.

Just then, an excited first-year student ran past, heading toward the common room. "Turn on the TV! Turn on the TV!" he called. "It's the Thunderbirds!"

Alan and Fermat glanced at each other and quickly followed the kid.

"What channel?" someone asked.

"Any channel!" the kid replied.

Alan smiled to himself. Thunderbird operations frequently preempted regular programming. As he and Fermat entered the common room, a huge crowd had already gathered around the big plasma-screen TV hanging on the wall. Barely able to see over the tops of the other students' heads, Alan and Fermat pushed their way toward the front of the crowd.

Lisa Lowe, a correspondent for International World Network, was reporting from a helicopter. Behind her, an oil-drilling rig as large as five football fields burned above a raging sea.

". . . disaster in the Bering Strait," Lisa Lowe reported with practiced calm. "Six workers remain trapped on the so-called super rig. Because of fire damage, the structure is in danger of total collapse. Only the Thunderbirds can avert what seems to be a tragedy in the making."

Something caught the reporter's eye. She turned and pointed, hope filling her voice. "And there they are!"

2

Thunderbirds in Action

The camera swung from Lisa Lowe and focused on the burning rig in the background. As the camera zoomed in, a swept-wing, rocket-like aircraft zoomed past. It was huge and impressive, if not nearly so massive as the flaming oil platform it circled. The sleek silver ship had a red nose-cone, blue trim, and the words THUNDERBIRD 1 stenciled in large letters along the side.

Thunderbird 1 banked to the left, using its VTOL (vertical takeoff and landing) engines to hold it steady as it surveyed the accident scene.

Alan, having finally pushed close to the TV, turned to Fermat and said, "They're going to need the equipment pod in *Thunderbird 2*."

As if on cue, a second Thunderbird arced into the picture. It was a massive green leviathan with small front-swept wings and a huge spoiler-like tailfin on the back. Two titanic rear-mounted engines flared, as *Thunderbird 2*'s turtle-shell-shaped fuselage swooped through the air toward the disaster.

"D—do you think they'll need *Thunderbird 4*?" Fermat whispered back.

Alan shook his head. "Not unless those workers end up in the water. Taking the sub in under that burning rig would be too dangerous otherwise."

"We've got a lot of turbulence up here," Lisa Lowe reported as the TV picture bounced badly, "but it looks like the Thunderbirds are going to attempt a rescue."

Thunderbird 2 swept low over the oil rig. The aircraft lurched violently and nearly collided with the platform as the updraft from the flames hit it. The assembled students gasped.

Thunderbird 1 continued to circle as *Thunderbird 2* hovered close to the crumbling rig. Six oil workers stood on a nearby scaffold, edging away from the smoke and flames.

"Come on, Dad!" Alan whispered.

A hatch opened in the belly of *Thunderbird 2*, and a small, circular escape lift lowered toward the trapped workers. A tall man in a silver Thunderbird flight uniform and helmet stood on the rescue platform.

"V—Virgil, do you think?" Fermat whispered. Alan nodded but didn't say anything. He was clutching the back of a nearby chair so tightly that his knuckles went white.

A huge wave slapped the side of the scaffold, and the oil rig lurched. The workers toppled off their feet and slid toward the brink.

Just as it seemed they would fall into the raging waters hundreds of feet below, six rescue lines shot out of the descending platform and clamped themselves around the workers.

Thunderbird 2 lurched up, towing Virgil and the six workers with it. The aircraft wheeled away from the burning wreck as a pylon buckled and the scaffold fell into the sea.

The assembled students cheered as *Thunderbird 2* winched the workers safely inside its armored fuselage.

"Unbelievable," Lisa Lowe said breathlessly. *Thunderbird 2* swooped away from the burning oil rig. "As always," she continued, "the Thunderbirds are working under a cloud of secrecy. We have no idea where the survivors will be taken for treatment. We do know, however, that none of them would have survived without the efforts of International Rescue. Though the world has come to depend on them, we still know precious little about these Thunderbirds."

"I bet they bring in *Thunderbird 3* to put out the fire," said Ian Welch. He hadn't been caught racing by the headmaster and had beaten Alan and Fermat to the common room.

Alan rolled his eyes. "*Thunderbird 3* is only used for extraorbital missions," he said. "It's actually not very maneuverable in the earth's atmosphere. They'll probably launch a rocket from *Thunderbird 1*."

Welch scowled at Alan. "Only an idiot would fight a fire with a rocket," he said. "What makes *you* such a Thunderbirds expert, anyway?"

Alan started to respond, but just at that moment, Fermat stomped down hard on his foot. Alan clamped his mouth shut.

Thunderbird 1 now streaked toward the blazing structure.

Alan imagined his father's voice commanding the operation from *Thunderbird 2*: "Commence knockdown procedure." And Virgil's response: "F.A.B." The media didn't have access to the Thunderbird communication frequencies, of course. Those were top secret, like everything else in the organization.

Thunderbird 1 swooped forward and fired a missile toward the geyser of flaming oil. The missile detonated directly over the blazing wellhead. The explosion filled the air with a cloud of smoke, sea water, and steam.

As the cloud surrounding the platform cleared, a black gusher of crude oil shot into the sky.

"The fire is out!" Lisa Lowe enthused. "The explosion at the wellhead robbed it of the oxygen it needed to burn—a classic oil fire-fighting tech- nique."

Alan shot a knowing grin at Ian Welch.

"Amazing!" Lowe continued. "The mysterious Thunderbirds have done it again!"

As the Thunderbirds arced away from the rig, the assembled students cheered resoundingly. "Yeeha!" Alan shouted, lifting Fermat in a big hug.

Welch rolled his eyes mockingly and made a lovesick face. "Oh, I wish *I* could be a Thunderbird one day!" he said, pretending to be Alan.

The boys around them laughed. Alan's face reddened with anger, but Welch didn't let up. "I hope you fly rockets better than you drive scooters, bird boy!" he said.

Alan stepped menacingly toward Welch. Welch clenched his fists, refusing to back down.

"Tracy!" barked Headmaster Tierney, appearing at the common room door. "Someone here to see you."

"Hello, boys," said a woman standing in the doorway. The afternoon sunlight flooded in from behind her, framing her perfect figure. She was tall, slender, and dressed in a short pink Chanel suit. All eyes turned toward her, and the room became very quiet.

"Lady Penelope," Alan said, surprised to see her.

The crowd parted in front of her as Penelope stepped into the room.

Ian Welch glanced at a magazine on a nearby coffee table. It featured Lady Penelope on the cover.

"You're . . . you're . . ." Welch began.

"Lady Penelope Creighton-Ward," she said, putting her hand affectionately on Alan's shoulder. She glanced at Welch. "And you're drooling, dear boy. Please do stop."

Welch clamped his mouth shut.

"Alan, darling," Penelope said, "I'm sorry to arrive on such short notice, but your father has been unexpectedly detained. He asked me to pick you up. Is that all right?"

Alan sighed, not wanting to reveal how thrilled he was to see his father's friend. "I suppose," he said casually.

"Fantastic!" she replied. "Now, will anyone be joining us for the spring holidays?"

Every hand in the room shot toward the ceiling, even Welch's. "Me! Me!" they all clamored. "Pick me!"

Alan shook his head. "Just Fermat."

Lady Penelope smiled her famous smile. "Quite right," she said.

Headmaster Tierney stepped forward nervously and cleared his throat. "Excuse me, your ladyship. You can save me a phone call to Mr. Tracy. You see, Alan had a bit of a discipline problem this morning . . . *again*."

"Run along to the car, you two," she said to Alan and Fermat. Then, turning her winning smile on Tierney, she asked, "Headmaster, do you think I could have just a tiny moment of your time?"

Alan smiled broadly at Lady Penelope as he and Fermat set their bags down on the sidewalk outside of their dorm. "I can't believe I'm not suspended," he said admiringly. "What did you say to him?"

"I complimented his thick, luxurious head of hair," Lady Penelope replied.

Alan and Fermat laughed. "Why are you in America, Lady Penelope?" Alan asked. "Are you on a mission?"

"Alan, shush! I am an *undercover* agent, after all. Please try to be discreet."

As she spoke, a six-wheeled, custom-built, pink limousine rolled up to the curb. The car was low and sleek, like a metal panther, and sported the license plate FAB 1 on its bumpers. Aloysius Parker, Lady Penelope's chauffeur, got out to help her into the car. He then loaded the boys' luggage into the rear.

"Hi, P—P—Parker," Fermat said.

The pug-faced former prizefighter shook Fermat's hand. His grip made the young inventor wince. "Good afternoon to you, Master Hackenbacker," Parker said.

"Hi, Nosey," Alan said.

Parker nodded affectionately at the youngest

Tracy. "Less of that attitude, young sir, or I shall be obliged to deliver the trademark Parker punch."

Alan grinned at him and put up his dukes. "Bring it on!" he said.

"No time for that," Lady Penelope said. "We're expected at the compound. Hop in, boys."

Alan and Fermat climbed into the pink limo, sitting three across in the enormous backseat with Lady Penelope. Parker got into the driver's seat, and they pulled down the driveway.

"Looking forward to spring break, Alan?" Penelope asked.

Alan sighed. "I *was,* but once my dad finds out about the scooter, I'm toast."

"Well, then," Lady Penelope said, "why don't you and I make it our little secret."

"You mean . . ." Alan said in disbelief. "Lady P., you are totally saving my butt!"

She smiled. "After all, we are a *rescue* organization."

Alan smiled back. "You are so cool!" he said. "Can I drive?"

Lady Penelope laughed—a light, musical sound—as Parker replied, "Don't press your luck."

They eased back into their seats as the car accelerated down the highway past a sign that read

Parker pressed some buttons on the dash, and a small, transparent screen dropped down from the brim of his cap. Data readouts and telemetry, like those in the cockpit of a fighter jet, spooled over the tiny screen. He made some final adjustments as the pink car rocketed down the highway.

Alan and Fermat glanced at each other. Parker was going far too fast to take the curve up ahead. They'd driven steadily upward since leaving the school and were now winding along the side of a steep cliff face.

Parker reached back and handed Lady Penelope her newspaper. "Lovely morning for a drive, milady."

"Isn't it just?" she said. "Mind the curve."

"No worries, milady," he replied.

He turned the wheel sharply to the left, and the Rolls shot off the cliff.

3

Home Not-So-Sweet Home

Alan and Fermat gripped the armrests as the custom car plunged toward the valley far below. A surge from *FAB 1*'s modified jet engines pushed them against their seats as the car sprouted wings.

The limo banked left, soaring effortlessly above the valley and into the clouds.

"Oh, listen, Parker, fantastic news," Lady Penelope said. She hadn't even looked up from her newspaper. "The economy has made a total recovery."

Parker kept his hands on the steering wheel as he guided *FAB 1* out of the clouds and over the water below. "I'm very glad to hear it, milady."

"And look—world peace at last," Lady Penelope continued.

"That is good news," Parker replied, nodding his head.

Lady Penelope turned the page. "Oh! And apparently England won the big match last night."

Parker lifted both hands off the wheel and cheered. *FAB 1* lurched left.

"Calm down, Parker," Lady Penelope said, playfully scolding him.

"Yes, milady."

Alan grinned broadly and high-fived Fermat. They were going home in style.

"Look, Mom, Thunderbirds!" The little boy's eyes lit up as he pointed to the night sky above the San Francisco hospital.

Thunderbirds 1 and *2* hung in the air a few feet over the hospital's helipad, their enormous bulks held aloft by powerful Hackenbacker-designed VTOL engines. A hatch opened in the belly of *Thunderbird 2*, and a platform, with the six rescued oil rig workers on it, dropped down toward the hospital staff waiting below. For security reasons, the Thunderbird pilots stayed inside their mighty ships.

One of the rescued workers, a huge bear of a man, leaned against the platform rail, looking weary from his ordeal.

Neither the doctors below nor the pilots above noticed the man pressing a secret switch on his belt. A tiny projectile shot out of his belt buckle and arced toward the sleek rocket hovering nearby.

The micromissile smashed into *Thunderbird 1*'s nose cone, splashing a small amount of fluorescent chemical on the ship's fuselage. The liquid quickly spread and seeped into the aircraft's metal skin.

As hospital workers helped the spy off the platform, a smile spread across his wicked face.

Unaware of his deception, the Thunderbirds raced away into the night.

Miles away, a submarine prowled beneath the surface of the Pacific Ocean. The sub had been built with advanced stealth technology, making it all but invisible to the world's superpowers and to International Rescue. A green light pulsed on the sub's tracking screen.

A bald-headed man wearing a deep red robelike garment embroidered with an elaborate dragon sat hunched over the command console. His piercing eyes focused on the screen and the ship now displayed on it.

"Ah, the chariot of the gods," he said, his voice smooth as silk and dark as a winter night. "Having dallied with mortals, they now return to Olympus." He watched the trajectory on the screen's map as *Thunderbird 1* streaked away from the west coast of America and over the Pacific Ocean. "Follow its flight path," he commanded the woman standing beside him.

Silently, the sub slipped through the deep—a shark pursuing its prey.

FAB 1 arced low over the South Pacific, the dawn sunlight splashing like fire over the car's sleek pink sides.

"Pardon me, milady," Parker said. "We are now on final approach to Tracy Island. Radar indicates we have some company."

Lady Penelope nodded. "Boys," she said, rousing Alan and Fermat, who were dozing on the seat beside her. As they woke, she pointed out the right-hand window.

The boys gazed over the dazzling waters below. At first, they didn't see anything. Then the flying car trembled, buffeted by a powerful gust of wind.

A loud roar filled the air as *Thunderbirds 1* and *2* swooped into formation alongside them.

Alan shouted and waved enthusiastically to the pilots. From the cockpit of *Thunderbird 2*, his father gave him a thumbs-up.

Then the great machines peeled away from *FAB 1* and shot ahead. Alan strained forward, watching them streak toward home. Then he slumped back against his seat, wishing that *he* were piloting one of the crafts rather than just watching them.

Even though he was the youngest, it didn't seem fair that he should be left out. One day, his dad and his brothers would see that he deserved to be a Thunderbird, too. Alan folded his arms across his chest and sulked as *FAB 1* made its final approach.

Tracy Island rose out of the ocean ahead of them. Its volcanic peak stretched toward the deep blue sky. Clouds drifted past the mountain's summit, and emerald jungles crept up the mountainside. Gentle waves lapped the sandy beaches circling the island.

A spectacular modern house—all glass and steel—sat perched on the mountainside near the shore. A large swimming pool stood at the home's base, and several smaller outbuildings dotted the pathways down to the beach. Palm trees, gently swaying in the breeze, lined the small, private runway. The Tracy home looked like an island paradise, but it secretly hid the headquarters of International Rescue.

Alan saw no sign of the Thunderbirds as they approached. The great machines must have already been stowed in their underground hangars. Alan fought down another twinge of envy for his brothers' work.

FAB 1 landed on the island's small airstrip. Parker unpacked as Alan, Fermat, and Lady Penelope headed up to the house. They found Alan's dad and the rest of the Thunderbirds team assembled in the kitchen, where Onaha—the Tracys' housekeeper—was whipping up dinner.

Jeff Tracy, a tall, ruggedly handsome man in his mid-forties, stood near one wall, chatting with Fermat's father, the man affectionately known by the team as "Brains." Fermat was the image of his father, right down to his oversized glasses.

"*Thunderbird 2* seemed a little twitchy out

there, Brains," Jeff Tracy was saying.

"Okay, Mr. T—Tracy," Brains said. "I'll s—study the flight data from the guidance processor."

Three of Alan's brothers bustled around the kitchen, sampling food and getting in Onaha's way. All were dressed casually, having changed out of their International Rescue gear upon returning home. Scott had sandy hair and intelligent features. Virgil was tall and lean, and quick with a joke or wisecrack. Gordon was just a few years older than Alan. The one brother not present, John, remained in space on *Thunderbird 5*.

". . . So then the oil pressure light comes on, and—" Gordon said, continuing a story.

Onaha cut him off. "Dinner is almost ready," she said. "Go! Sit!" She tried to usher the boys toward the dining room. Spotting Alan and Fermat in the doorway, she flashed them a smile.

"Hey, Alan!" Jeff Tracy said, heading toward his youngest son.

"Dad!" Alan replied.

"P—Pop!" said Fermat.

"F—Fer— son!" Brains stuttered.

Both boys crossed the kitchen and gave their fathers big hugs.

Each of Alan's brothers paused on his way to the

dining room long enough to tousle Alan's hair.

"Hey, sprout."

"Hey, buddy."

"Virgil, Scott," Alan said, getting more annoyed with each ruffle.

"Hey, chief," Gordon said, reaching for Alan's head.

Alan glared at him. "Don't even *think* about it." All three older brothers laughed.

As they sat down and began eating, Alan said, "I saw the mission on TV, Dad. It looked pretty dangerous."

"It's always dangerous, son," Jeff replied. "But it's what we do."

"Do you think the fire was causing updrafts? That would explain—"

"Enough shop talk," Jeff Tracy interrupted. "I want to hear about school."

Alan frowned. "School's boring."

His dad smiled indulgently. "Hey, no school, no rockets. No rockets, no Thunderbirds. You've got to walk before you can fly, son."

"So then I get this wind-shear reading telling me it's blowing sixty knots," Scott said, continuing his earlier conversation with Gordon and Virgil.

"No way," Virgil countered.

"Did you try readjusting the flaps?" Alan asked, eager to join in.

"First thing I did, sprout," Scott replied. "It's not my first day in a Thunderbird, you know."

"*Try* to keep up," Gordon said, rolling his eyes at Alan.

"Don't you have homework to do or something?" Virgil asked.

"Unless he's blown up this school like the last one," Gordon added.

"It was just the science lab!" Alan protested. His brothers laughed.

"That's enough, boys," Jeff Tracy said.

"Alan," Onaha said pleasantly, "you haven't touched your food. Eat! Eat!"

"I'm not hungry," Alan replied angrily. "Come on, Fermat." He pushed his plate away and dashed out the door.

4

Under Fire

Fermat glanced at his dad. Brains nodded, and Fermat rushed after his friend.

Jeff Tracy put down his fork and scowled at his older sons, all of whom shrugged.

"Alan, wait," Jeff called. "Come back." He rose from the table and hurried after his youngest son. By the time Jeff got outside, though, Fermat and Alan had already disappeared.

Kyrano, who was in charge of the house and grounds with his wife, Onaha, stood tending some flower beds nearby. "Have you seen Alan?" Jeff asked. "His brothers were teasing him again. He ran off with Fermat."

Kyrano shook his head. "I have not seen either one." He snipped off an exquisite flower and handed it to Jeff. "For Lady Penelope," Kyrano explained. "You should ask her, perhaps."

Jeff glanced toward the pool deck below. Lady Penelope lay stretched out on a lounge chair, enjoying the sun and sipping a drink. Jeff hiked down the stairway and presented the flower to her.

"Kyrano wanted me to give it to you," Jeff said.

Penelope took the bloom, her eyes twinkling behind her sunglasses. She slid the flower into her hair and asked, "How do I look?"

Jeff was at a loss for words. She always looked more beautiful than he could express. "You look . . ." he began.

Penelope's cell phone rang. "Hold that thought," she said, and then spoke into the receiver. "Yes, Parker . . . Thank you. I'll be right there." She rose from the lounge chair. "I have to go," she said gravely. "It seems that fire at the oil rig was no accident."

"Any suspects?" Jeff asked.

"Not yet, but I'll keep you posted," she replied.

"Always saving the world," he said with a smile.

She smiled in return. "I learned from the best.

Now, you were saying . . . ?"

"Hey, Mr. Tracy!" called a girl's voice. Kyrano and Onaha's daughter, Tin-Tin, dashed up toward the house from the beach. She was Alan's age, athletic, and good-looking. She wore a surfing bodysuit, sandals, and a seashell barrette in her hair. A shining golden crystal hung on a chain around her neck. "Good evening, Lady Penelope," she said.

"Hello, Tin-Tin. That necklace looks beautiful on you."

Tin-Tin blushed. "Thanks."

"Tin-Tin, did you know Alan's back?" Jeff asked.

Tin-Tin frowned. "Alan's back?" she said. Her tone made it clear that she wasn't completely thrilled by the news. "If I see him, I'll tell him you're looking for him." She hurried up the steps to see her dad.

Jeff shook his head. "When are those two going to get along?"

"Well," Lady Penelope said, "girls are generally ahead of boys with this type of thing."

Jeff looked puzzled. "What type of thing?"

"Romance," Penelope replied.

"Alan and Tin-Tin?" Jeff asked. "I didn't see *that* coming." He chuckled and shook his head.

"No, you wouldn't," Penelope said sweetly. "I must run. Good luck finding Alan."

She headed for the airstrip while Jeff jogged away in the opposite direction.

Alan gazed at the incredible miniaturized control systems arrayed before him. "Okay, Fermat, run preflight checks."

Sitting in the cockpit of *Thunderbird 1* beside Alan, Fermat gazed rapturously over the dials and switches. It was hard to believe that their fathers had designed and built such amazing machines.

Fermat adopted an official flight crew voice and said, "Hydraulic systems are g—g—green."

Alan nodded. "Commence main engine sequence."

Fermat leaned forward and pretended to flick a switch. "F.A.B., Alan."

Alan rubbed his hands in anticipation. "It couldn't hurt just to fire up the instruments," he said. He reached for a switch on the control panel.

"Alan, that's the—" Fermat began.

Alan hit the switch and the cockpit suddenly lit up. Dials and instrument panels glowed, lights flashed in programmed sequences, and the onboard computer system whirred to life.

"—wrong switch!" Fermat finished, despairingly.

Alan began flipping switches, trying desperately to turn everything off. Fermat did the same.

"Could this day get any worse?" Alan asked rhetorically.

Jeff Tracy's stern face appeared on the ship's main monitor. "Alan, my office. *Now.* Fermat, your father would like to have a word with you."

Alan and Fermat stepped out of the huge rocket onto the service gantry. As the massive craft dropped away from them toward the floor of the silo, Fermat said, "We are so b—b—busted."

Alan gazed longingly at *Thunderbird 1*, knowing neither he nor Fermat were likely to be allowed near it again any time soon. His eyes downcast, he started to follow Fermat out of the Silo. Fermat stopped suddenly, and Alan crashed into him.

"Hey, look at this," Fermat said. He pointed to a strange, glittering substance on the ship's fuselage.

"What is it?" Alan asked, glad of any excuse to delay going to his father's office.

Fermat pulled a cotton swab from his jacket pocket and took a sample of the mysterious substance. "L—looks like a g—gallium electrolyte compound."

Alan frowned. "Who would put something like that on *Thunderbird 1*?"

Jeff Tracy rose from the chair behind his desk and stared out the huge glass windows lining the oceanside wall of his office. Behind him, a line of large photo portraits of himself and his older sons—the Thunderbirds team—hung on the wall. A smaller photo of Alan sat atop his desk along with other family pictures.

Jeff turned as Alan, red-faced and excited, burst into the room.

"Dad, I know you're mad," Alan began. "I shouldn't have been in the ship. But we found—"

"No," Jeff said angrily. "I don't care what the excuse is. You're grounded for the rest of spring break. There's a reason you're not allowed in the cockpit by yourself. You're not ready. What you did was incredibly dangerous."

"But nothing happened, Dad. I had it under control!"

"Oh, really? You started a Thunderbird without putting up the anti-detection shield—potentially revealing our location and identity." He leaned his palms on his desk and stared into Alan's eyes. "If you want to be part of the team, you have to follow the rules. You put everyone in danger when you act selfishly. Understand?"

"I understand," Alan said angrily. "I understand that you don't want me to be a Thunderbird. You don't want me to do anything. You won't even listen when I'm trying to tell you something important."

"Bottom line, Alan," Jeff said with forced calm, "before you have any chance of being a Thunderbird, you need to grow up."

"Then let me!" Alan shouted as he ran from the office.

"Alan—" Jeff started, but his youngest son was already out of earshot.

Jeff chided himself silently. He'd been too rough on the boy. Maybe he was too rough on all of them, but in their line of work they couldn't afford mistakes.

He sat down behind his desk, idly picking up a picture from years ago, when they'd all been together, even his wife. A feeling of deep sadness stole over Jeff as he watched the spectacular sunset outside his window. He sat there alone for a long time as dark shadows crept across the floor of the room.

Jeff had nearly dozed off when an electronic chime broke his reverie. He turned toward the line of portraits hung on the wall. The picture of John, his eldest son, had been replaced with a live video feed. John was currently manning *Thunderbird 5*, International Rescue's secret space station. Behind John, lights flashed on huge panels containing the most sophisticated sensing, surveillance, and communications equipment that money could buy.

"John, how are you?" Jeff asked.

"Good," John replied. "But I could use a pizza. Do you know a place that delivers?"

Jeff laughed. "Anything else on your mind?"

John checked a few nearby monitors. "Forest fire in Vladivostok, typhoon heading for Singapore . . . and Lucy's landed herself in a heap of trouble." He indicated a black-and-white image from an old TV show.

"I think the local authorities can handle that— and most of the other stuff, too. Keep your eyes open, though."

"F.A.B.," John replied, giving the Thunderbirds signal for "Understood." Then, looking more closely at his father across the telelink, he asked,

"So what's happening on planet Tracy?"

"Alan's home," Jeff said with a sigh. "Some-times I wonder if I did the right thing, raising you boys here alone. Alan's had such a hard time of it since . . ."

"Dad, you did a great job. That doesn't mean we don't all miss Mom sometimes. Don't worry, Alan will pull through this. All of us have before."

Jeff Tracy nodded. "Thanks, John."

"F.A.B., Dad. Over and out." John's portrait returned to normal.

As dawn crept across the Pacific, the muscular spy who had fired the gallium compound at *Thunderbird 1* peered through the periscope of The Hood's submarine. "The island is in sight," he said.

The Hood nodded. "Very good, Mullion." He pressed a button on a nearby console. "Transom, I need you."

A moment later, a young woman in skin-tight pants and a black shirt arrived in the control room. She was curved and muscular in just the right proportions, physically lovely, save for her huge black glasses and a set of very bad teeth.

"We have a positive visual from the tracking

solution on *Thunderbird 1*," Transom said.

"Missiles?" asked The Hood.

"Armed and ready, sir," Mullion replied. "Should I target the island's main structure?"

"Why would I want to destroy what will soon be mine?" The Hood asked. "In the East, we're taught to use an opponent's strength against him." He stared at the larger man. "Notice how easily I root you where you stand."

Mullion scoffed but, with The Hood's glowing eyes upon him, he found he could not move.

The Hood smiled. "It would be almost impossible to force the Thunderbirds to leave their island. On the other hand, it requires no effort at all to let them go. The Thunderbirds' purpose is to rescue. All we need is to give them a victim. Commence target triangulation," he said to Transom.

Transom pushed a few buttons at her work station. "Target acquisition of *Thunderbird 5* is locked," she replied.

The Hood closed his eyes and whispered, "Fire!"

5

Deep Trouble

Just before sunrise, Fermat crept down to the lab to check on his father. The young scientist had been sent to bed early for his part in starting up *Thunderbird 1*. He hadn't slept well, and now he realized why.

"Hey, son," Brains said as Fermat entered the room, "is it bedtime already?" The genius who built the Thunderbirds sat hunkered over some delicate electronic equipment in one corner of the operations hangar.

"It's almost dawn, Dad," Fermat replied. "You've been working all night."

Brains smiled wistfully.

"Dad," Fermat said, "I need to tell you some-thing."

"What's the matter, son?"

"Alan and I found some sort of gallium com-pound on the fuselage of *Thunderbird 1*."

"That could be important," Brains said. "Let's check it out r—ri— immediately." He put his arm around his son's shoulder, and they left the lab together.

The Hood's missile burst from the water and into the morning air. The stealth properties of the weapon rendered it invisible to electronic detec-tion; radar could not spot it. Alan Tracy might have seen the launch, but he was busy sulking on the island's far beach.

As the missile arced into the upper atmosphere, its beautiful serrated wings unfurled. It began to spin as it approached its target.

Within seconds, the missile tore through the outer ring of *Thunderbird 5,* and a terrible explosion shook the space station. The impact knocked John Tracy from his seat, throwing him against an instrument panel. *Thunderbird 5*'s emergency lights flashed on, and alarms howled a belated warning.

John struggled to his feet. His left arm ached terribly. His head throbbed, and spots danced before his eyes. He concentrated, willing himself not to black out.

The monitor screens surrounding him showed only bad news: hull breach . . . loss of atmosphere . . . auto-repair systems negative.

Sparks flew from *Thunderbird 5*'s control panels. Smoke billowed from the circuits and fires flared around the room.

John hit the communications equipment with his good hand. "*Thunderbird 5* to Tracy Island. Mayday! Mayday!"

Miles below, Brains and Fermat heard the emergency signal and raced to Jeff's office to answer the call.

Brains jumped behind Jeff's desk and pressed a series of hidden buttons. "Switching to command and control center," he said.

As he spoke, the office transformed itself into the headquarters of International Rescue. Modern chairs and furniture folded and disappeared into trapdoors. The huge desk pivoted into the floor to be replaced by a high-tech command console. Pictures on the wall became giant monitors. Huge banks of computer equipment rose from the floor and descended from hidden panels in the ceiling. Massive steel blast shutters slid shut across the picture windows.

As the transformation finished, Jeff Tracy and his three older sons rushed in. Jeff, Virgil, Scott, and Gordon took up positions in front of their portraits on the wall.

"How bad is it, Brains?" Jeff asked.

Brains scanned the surrounding displays. "Major damage to *Thunderbird 5*. Possible m—meteor strike."

"I'll t—tell Alan!" Fermat said, sprinting from the room.

"Thunderbirds are *go*!" Jeff commanded. As he spoke, the portraits behind the team changed, morphing into pictures of the Tracys in their International Rescue uniforms. The wall behind them flipped back, sending them down the launch chutes to the hangar.

Jeff and his sons boarded *Thunderbird 3* and hurried to prepare for blastoff.

Alan stood on a boulder at the ocean's edge and pointed his stone skimmer out across the water. He pulled the trigger, and a disk-shaped stone shot out of the end of the device and skipped across the waves. He counted twelve hops—a new record—but it didn't make him feel any better.

Suddenly, the water in front of him surged and a figure sprang at him. Alan jumped back in alarm, tripped, and ended up on his backside.

Tin-Tin pulled off her mask and snorkel, and laughed as she waded toward him. She had a diver's knife tucked into her belt and a string bag full of shells in her hand. "Scared you!" she said playfully.

Alan rose and dusted himself off. "That wasn't funny."

"What's the matter, Alan? Don't you like to play with girls?"

"Sure," he shot back. "Know any?"

A thundering roar shook the air as *Thunderbird 3* rocketed into the morning sky. Alan and Tin-Tin stopped bickering and watched the big machine disappear into the heavens.

"Alan! Alan!" called Fermat, running up to them. "*Thunderbird 5* has been hit! John's in real t—t—trouble! Your dad and brothers have gone to help."

Alan's and Tin-Tin's eyes went wide with shock.

Quickly mastering his emotions, Alan said,

"Don't panic. International Rescue can handle this."

As he spoke, the ocean behind them boiled, and a huge submarine burst to the surface. It breached like a whale and crashed into the surf, headed straight for the beach.

"On the other hand . . ." Alan said. "Run!"

6

In Control

In the darkness of the submarine, The Hood watched as *Thunderbird 3* shot into the stratosphere. Then a hatch overhead opened, and sunlight streamed in.

Mullion stuck his head in through the hatch. "We've made land," he announced.

Transom flicked a switch at her console, and the sub's forward observation windows opened. She stood and gazed at the island—the verdant jungle, the towering volcano, the pristine beaches, the magnificent modern buildings. "It's beautiful," she said, taking it all in.

A butterfly fluttered down through the hatch.

The Hood glanced at it. It twitched once and then fell to the desk, stunned. "Cut them off," he commanded.

Transom returned to her station and threw another switch. "Communications blackout activated," she said. "They'll never know what hit them."

"Of course they will," The Hood replied. "As soon as we tell them." He headed for the topside hatch. "Come. Our prize awaits." Transom, Mullion, and The Hood's private army followed him out of the sub.

Jeff Tracy punched commands into the computer of *Thunderbird 3* and held tight to the control stick. *Thunderbird 5* floated within sight now. Debris from the impact hung around the space station like a glittering halo. The station wobbled precariously, its orbit disrupted by the catastrophe.

Virgil, Gordon, and Scott worked with their father as Jeff guided the rocket in.

John's voice crackled over the radio. "I'm losing all power. Generators are down."

"Hold on, son," Jeff said. "We're coming." He angled the huge rocket toward the docking port on the side of the station.

"*Thunderbird 5*'s gyros aren't working properly," Scott said. "The docking computer can't get a lock."

Grim determination settled on Jeff Tracy's face. "Then we'll do this the old-fashioned way. Hang on, boys."

He took manual control of the retro-rockets and guided *Thunderbird 3* with the control stick. He lined up the ships' docking ports and moved in slowly, matching the space station's wobble and spin.

For a moment, it seemed the two ships would collide. Jeff pulled back on the stick and turned slightly to starboard. "Now, Scott! Now!" he said.

Scott activated the docking mechanism.

With a whir and a grinding clunk, the two air-locks met and linked.

"We're in!" Gordon said triumphantly.

"Not yet we aren't," Virgil cautioned. "But we are locked on."

"Take the emergency packs, boys," Jeff said. "We're going in." He and the rest grabbed their equipment and headed to *Thunderbird 3*'s airlock.

Moments later, the doors mating the two ships opened and all four of them clambered into *Thunderbird 5*. Smoke and sparks surrounded them. Lights flashed in the darkness and emergency klaxons blared.

John struggled toward them, leaning on a bulkhead for support. "Am I glad to see you guys!" he gasped.

"You're hurt," Jeff said. "Virgil, take care of John. Scott, tackle the fires. Gordon, work on the oxygen systems. I'll see what I can do to stabilize this bird. Let's move!"

Alan, Fermat, and Tin-Tin watched as The Hood and his cronies strode toward the Tracy compound.

"How'd they find the island?" Alan asked, worried. "Was it what I did in *Thunderbird 1*?"

"N—no," Fermat replied. "My preliminary analysis of the compound we discovered on the side of the ship suggests that it might have some kind of transmitting capability."

"We need to warn Mr. Tracy and the others," Tin-Tin said.

"My dad is in the control room," Fermat noted. "But how do we g—g—get there now?"

Alan looked around, his brain racing. The invaders and their submarine had cut off the kids from the complex. He tried to think of a way they could get into the control room, but his mind was completely blank. He looked around, panic building inside him.

"The vents!" he said suddenly, pointing to one of the big intakes hidden in the foliage nearby. "We can use the vents."

Alan, Fermat, and Tin-Tin dashed for the opening and pried off the cover.

"Intruder alert! Intruder alert!" the instrument panels lining the control room blared. Brains wasn't ignoring the warnings, but they weren't the most pressing thing on his mind. He was concentrating on the rescue of *Thunderbird 5*.

"What is wrong with these instruments?" Brains asked. He threw switches and worked frantically at the consoles. "Mr. Tracy, do you copy? *Thunderbird 3*, please respond!"

He banged his fist on the desk in frustration, but no reply came.

"Oh, n—no!" he gasped, spotting the heavily armed marauders on one of the compound's security monitors. Brains Hackenbacker had every confidence that the control room's armored windows would hold. He had designed them himself and supervised their construction.

Nevertheless, concealing the headquarters of International Rescue remained a priority. With a flip of a switch, the room transformed from high-tech control room back into Jeff Tracy's office.

Brains seated himself at Jeff's computer console and tried to reach *Thunderbirds 3* and *5* again. "Jeff . . . Scott . . . c—come in!"

An explosion shook the reinforced-steel door. Brains ducked as the door's handle and latching mechanism flew past his head.

Before Brains could recover, Mullion charged in and threw the brilliant scientist to the floor. The Hood, Transom, and a number of armed guards followed Mullion into the room.

"Wh—wh—who are you?" Brains gasped, reeling from the blow.

"The more important question," said The Hood, his voice purring smoothly, "is who are *you*? Who is behind the Thunderbirds?" The villain's flashing eyes scanned the room, finally coming to rest on the portraits of Jeff Tracy and his boys.

The Hood smiled. "Jeff Tracy, the billionaire ex-astronaut. Of course. Didn't he lose his wife in an accident? How tragic."

Transom, who had been examining the room, suddenly stopped and gawked at Brains.

"Professor Hackenbacker?" she asked.

Brains nodded woozily.

"We met at last year's international conference on nanotechnology. I thought your thesis on neutrinos was extremely stimulating." She smiled at him, almost bashfully.

Brains pushed his thick-rimmed glasses up on his nose and blinked, trying to chase the spots from his eyes. Transom stooped to help him up.

"Transom," The Hood said, "concentrate on the task at hand."

Transom left Brains on the floor and pulled a handheld scanner from her belt. "Sorry, sir. The command control system is here," she said. "It's a fingerprint recognition system."

The Hood turned to gaze at Brains, still slumped on the floor. "Professor, please activate the control switch."

"N—n—never," Brains replied.

Mullion dragged the scientist to his feet and held him in front of The Hood.

"Professor, you and I share an interest in the science of the mind," The Hood said calmly. "But even the strongest mind can be broken. It would be a shame to break yours."

"F—f—forget it!" Brains shot back.

The Hood stared at Brains. The villain's eyes seemed to pulsate and flash. His pupils grew larger and then smaller. "Activate the control switch, professor," he said.

Brains stared back, trying to fight The Hood's evil influence. Then his body jerked and he began to walk forward, slowly, hesitatingly. The brilliant scientist tottered from side to side, struggling just to maintain his balance.

Mullion laughed. "Look at him! Just like a puppet on a string!"

Brains moved toward the desk. He looked at his fingers, trying to will them not to do what The Hood wanted. It was no use. He flicked a switch, and a palm-recognition plate slid out from beneath the desk.

He pressed his hand into it, and once again the room transformed into the high-tech headquarters of International Rescue.

Transom smiled, showing her crooked teeth. "We have control!"

7

Rescue Required

Red emergency beacons blinked rapidly, filling the smoky space station with eerie light. Jeff and his boys had fought down most of the fires, but they weren't out of trouble yet, not by a long shot.

John sat woozily against one wall, having his arm bandaged by Virgil.

"How is he?" Jeff asked, not pausing his work at the control console.

"He's been better," Virgil replied.

"I could still use that pizza," John said dreamily.

Suddenly, another warning light flared. Jeff looked around, reluctant to abandon the station.

He took a deep breath. "Back to *Thunderbird 3* . . . *now*!"

The four brothers and their dad hustled down the airlock corridor. Jeff helped John as they made their way toward the docked spaceship.

Scott arrived at the far end first and punched the entry sequence into the keypad on the door. Nothing happened. He tried again. Still, nothing.

"The locking mechanism is jammed!" Scott yelled.

Lights flickered and then brightened as power in the airlock switched back on.

"What's going on here?" Jeff asked angrily.

A viewscreen on the side of the corridor flickered to life, and the menacing visage of The Hood appeared.

"Attention, *Thunderbird 5*," he said. "As you can see, I have taken over your facilities. You no longer control your operational systems." He turned to Transom and said, "Warm them up, Transom."

Transom smiled toothily into the camera and punched some buttons on her control panel. "If you Thunderbirds begin to feel a bit toasty in a few minutes, don't worry," she said. "It's only because you're reentering the atmosphere. Please sit back and enjoy the ride. It won't last long."

Then Kyrano and Onaha were brought in to Jeff's office and shoved next to Brains. The Hood turned toward Kyrano.

Kyrano's eyes went wide, and he uttered a single word, "You . . . !" Then he collapsed to the floor, grabbing his head in pain.

Jeff fought back the rage welling up inside him and spoke calmly into the video link. "I'm willing to talk about your demands, but first of all, tell me who you are."

The Hood chuckled slightly. "Oh, how rude of me. You can call me The Hood. Now, listen. We aren't negotiating, Mr. Tracy. You're only alive because I want you to see me destroy in ten hours what it took you ten years to build. I'm going to use the Thunderbirds to rob the largest banks in the world." He walked to Jeff's desk and indicated a spinning holographic model of the earth. "Starting with the Bank of England." As he spoke, ten cities on the globe lit up. "The world's monetary system will be thrown into chaos, and the Thunderbirds will be held responsible."

"The Thunderbirds were designed to save lives," Jeff said, his anger nearly boiling over.

The Hood approached the camera, his eyes flashing. "Perhaps you have forgotten me, but surely you remember saving the life of my brother, Kyrano."

For a moment, Jeff and the Thunderbirds were too stunned to say anything.

Kyrano struggled to his feet. "I'm sorry, Mr. Tracy," he said.

"You left me to die that day," The Hood continued. "Well, you may have broken my body, but you have no idea how powerful my mind has become. Now you will suffer as I suffered, waiting for a rescue that will never come."

He flicked off the viewscreen, leaving Jeff and the boys alone in *Thunderbird 5.*

"How'd this joker find the island?" Virgil asked angrily.

"I don't know," Jeff replied, pounding his fist against the wall, "but this is exactly why I've kept our identities top secret. If he takes control of the Thunderbirds . . ."

"No one can stop him," Virgil said, finishing his father's thought.

Jeff went to where Scott and Gordon were working on a bank of circuitry.

"We've managed to wire in the oxygen scrubber

to the emergency batteries," Scott said.

"How long will it buy us?" Jeff asked.

Gordon shook his head. "I'm not sure."

"Four hours max," John said. Then he checked a monitor. "And gravity is deteriorating."

In the ventilation duct behind the International Rescue control room, Alan Tracy took his ear away from the wall behind the Tracy portraits and said, "Whoa!"

"Our parents are being held captive by my long lost *uncle*?" Tin-Tin asked incredulously. "I heard Lady Penelope telling your dad about her new case. Maybe this guy has something to do with that."

"C—co—cou . . . ka-choo!" Fermat sneezed. "S—sorry!" he whispered. "These vents are murder on my allergies."

"That's okay," Alan whispered back. "I don't think they heard us."

As he put his ear to the wall again, Mullion's huge fist slammed through the picture-screen next to him. Plastic plasma tubes, computer chips, and microwires flew everywhere as Mullion grabbed for Alan.

"Time to go," Alan said, ducking.

Before he could run, though, Mullion seized the back of his shirt. Fermat and Tin-Tin grabbed Alan's arms and yanked hard. Mullion lurched forward as the teens pulled his head and arms through the wall into the service tunnel. Mullion sneered and redoubled his efforts. Slowly but surely, he began to drag Alan back toward the control room.

Desperate, Tin-Tin lunged forward and sank her teeth into Mullion's hand. The big hoodlum bellowed in pain and let go.

Alan, Tin-Tin, and Fermat turned and dived into the nearby launch chutes. They shot down the slide, heading for the underground Thunderbirds hangar.

On the other side of the wall, Mullion rubbed his wounded hand.

The Hood glared at him, and the big man staggered back, as though physically struck.

"Apparently," The Hood said venomously, "the island is not as secure as you thought."

He grabbed a picture showing the Tracy family, their staff, and their children off Jeff's desk.

"Children!" The Hood snapped. "When you swept the compound did you find any children?"

He glared at Mullion again. The big man staggered back again.

Transom, working at one of the monitors, brought up a picture of Alan, Fermat, and Tin-Tin running through an underground hangar.

"Here they are," she said. *"Thunderbird 2*'s silo."

The Hood nodded. "Seal them in."

"Alan, the doors!" Tin-Tin cried.

Ahead of them, the big blast doors leading to *Thunderbird 3*'s hangar were sliding shut.

"This way," Alan called, changing direction as the first doors clanged shut. They all raced toward a second set, but those, too, closed before they could reach them.

"They've got us trapped!" Tin-Tin said.

"If we can get into *Thunderbird 1*'s silo, we can escape through the service t—t—tunnel," Fermat said.

"I'll handle the door," Alan said confidently. "You use the *Firefly* to take care of the goons." He pointed toward an eight-wheeled firefighting truck topped with a powerful-looking cannon.

"B—but these machines are only to be used for emergencies," Fermat said. Then he quickly added, "I guess this qu—qu—qualifies."

He and Tin-Tin ran to the *Firefly* while Alan ducked into an equipment pod stationed near *Thunderbird 2*. As Tin-Tin climbed into the *Firefly*, she saw the elevator doors begin to open. "Here they come!" she called.

Fermat started the huge machine's engine. The *Firefly* lurched forward. Tin-Tin fell from her seat. "Hey! Watch it!"

"I took microbiology instead of driver's ed," Fermat explained. As Tin-Tin regained her seat, he spun the machine toward the elevator doors.

Just then the *Thunderizer*, a big cannonlike rover, burst out of a nearby equipment pod. Alan drove it toward the far door just as The Hood's men entered through the elevator doors opposite.

Mullion strode confidently through the portal, leading a band of The Hood's troops.

"Five hundred PSI should do it," Tin-Tin said. She adjusted the pressure dial and took aim with the Firefly's foam cannon.

"Retreat!" Mullion yelled, seeing their peril. Before he could react, a huge jet of flame-retardant foam sprayed out, blasting the invaders back into the elevator.

As the villains floundered, Alan took aim with

the *Thunderizer*, a rescue machine designed to blast through obstructions without harming trapped people. The muzzle of the Thunderizer's cannon glowed green as charged particles built up within its barrel.

Voom!

A scintillating ball of green energy burst from the cannon, blowing a hole straight through the doors into *Thunderbird 1*'s hangar.

"Come on!" Alan called, leaping from the machine and running for the door. The others climbed down from the *Firefly* and dashed after him.

"Where's Fermat?" Alan asked as he and Tin-Tin ducked through the hole. They glanced back, but saw only Mullion's thugs tearing at the rapidly hardening foam.

"Coming!" Fermat called, sprinting toward them from behind *Thunderbird 2*.

"What were you doing back there?" Alan asked as they raced ahead.

"I had an id—id—dea . . ." Fermat replied.

"Well, try to keep up," Alan said. "Yell when you see them coming," he told Tin-Tin. "I'll open the tunnel."

He dashed to the service tunnel door and began

punching in the entry code. He smiled, his fingers flying over the keypad. "That should just about do—"

Alan stopped in midsentence and gasped.

On the other side of the door waited The Hood.

8

The Master Plan

Only the service tunnel door's safety glass separated Alan from his enemy.

Alan.

The youngest Tracy heard the voice, but he didn't see The Hood's lips move. A cold lump formed in the bottom of Alan's stomach.

Were you surprised to hear what your father did to me? The Hood asked telepathically. *It's frightening when we realize our parents aren't perfect.* He paused. *But perhaps you already suspected that about your father.*

Alan tried to resist, but he found his eyes drawn to The Hood's eerie gaze.

Why did your father build these magnificent machines? The Hood continued. *Do you suppose it was guilt, Alan? Because he let your mother die?*

Alan's mind reeled, and the lump in his stomach turned to a burning coal. Sweat poured down his forehead. Could it be true? Had his father let his mother die?

The Hood smiled pleasantly. *Open the door, Alan.*

Alan leaned toward the keypad. How easy it would be to just punch in the final numbers.

Open the door.

With a supreme effort, Alan shook his head and turned away from the door. Then he backed toward the base of *Thunderbird 1* with Fermat and Tin-Tin. The mighty rocket stood in launch position over closed blast doors that vented its exhaust out of the hangar bay.

They glanced back the way they'd come. In the next room, Mullion and his thugs had broken free at last. A hiss of air from the other direction told them that The Hood had discovered how to open the service door without Alan's help.

"Alan! What do we do?" Fermat asked, trying to squelch the panic in his voice.

"I'm thinking!" Alan shot back. They'd backed

up against the fins of *Thunderbird 1* and didn't have any place to retreat.

Alan looked frantically around the hangar—the ship, the catwalks arcing high above, the gantry, and the floor. Inspiration struck! He pulled the stone skimmer from his back pocket, loaded a stone into it, and pointed it at The Hood.

"That toy won't do us any good," Tin-Tin cried.

Alan fired the rock at the villain.

The Hood swayed to one side and the stone fell harmlessly to the floor. He smiled as he walked toward the children. "It's not me you're angry at, Alan," he said.

Alan loaded another stone. "It's not you I'm aiming at, either."

He fired again. The rock whizzed past The Hood and smashed into a large button on the wall.

"Get them!" The Hood commanded.

Before Mullion could grab any of them, the vent doors beneath *Thunderbird 1* swung open. Alan, Fermat, and Tin-Tin dropped into the exhaust tube and disappeared.

Mullion skidded to a stop at the edge of the pit. He pulled a walkie-talkie from his belt. "Transom," he said, "fire up the engines on *Thunderbird 1*. Set to broil."

The Hood and his minions backed away as Transom flicked switches in the control room. *Thunderbird 1*'s engines roared to life, belching huge gusts of orange flame into the exhaust tube.

Sliding down the tube, Alan, Tin-Tin, and Fermat heard the blast of *Thunderbird 1*'s engines behind them. They looked back. A wall of fire zoomed toward them.

Suddenly, the chute dropped out from under them as they reached the exhaust port. The roaring flames passed harmlessly overhead as Alan, Tin-Tin, and Fermat plunged toward the Pacific Ocean, sixty feet below.

They hit the water hard, sending spray and foam high into the air. Then the ocean closed over their heads, swallowing them whole.

In the control room, Transom worked the surveillance systems monitoring the island. She looked up as The Hood and Mullion entered the room. "No sign of them, sir," she said.

"Of course not," Mullion boasted. "The little brats went up like firecrackers—Pop! Pop! Pop!" He laughed.

Brains lunged forward. "You b—b—b—rat!"

Mullion turned to pound him, but a glance from The Hood stopped Brains dead in his tracks.

"Don't give him the satisfaction of beating you, professor," The Hood said calmly.

Brains collapsed to the ground, holding his head in his hands.

"This has taken far too long," The Hood said. "Mullion, pick out the equipment you need to get into those banks and load it into *Thunderbird 2*. No more delays. We wouldn't want Jeff Tracy and the remainder of his brood to burn up before the show."

Alan and Tin-Tin burst to the surface of the hidden lagoon near the exhaust chute. The cove wasn't a very far walk from the cliff, but it was a long way to swim without taking a breath.

"Made it!" Alan said.

"Guess those diving lessons finally paid off," added Tin-Tin.

Alan looked around. "Where's Fermat?" he asked. Seeing no sign of the young scientist, he swam around frantically, calling, "Fermat! Fermat!"

Tin-Tin took a deep breath and dived back under. Her lithe form disappeared into the depths, back the way they'd come. As Alan considered diving after her, she resurfaced near the lagoon entrance, towing Fermat in her arms.

Fermat coughed and sputtered as she dragged him toward shore. "How about a little warning the next time you pull a s—stunt like that?" he asked.

"Sure," Alan replied. "I'll remember that next time Tin-Tin's uncle takes over International Rescue and tries to kill us all."

They clambered ashore and found some bushes behind which they could wring out their wet clothes. Tin-Tin scouted the area for intruders.

"How was I supposed to know you couldn't swim?" Alan asked Fermat. "We live on an *island*."

"I t—t—took organic chemistry instead of swimming lessons," Fermat replied.

"Next time, double up," Alan suggested. Then, seeing his friend's hurt look, he said. "I'm sorry, Fermat. Forget it. Let's figure out how to get out of this fix. We need to be ready for anything."

"Boo!"

Alan and Fermat jumped. Tin-Tin, who had sneaked up behind them, laughed. The boys scowled at her and quickly pulled their wrung out clothes back on over their underwear.

"So I was thinking," Alan said, fighting down embarrassment, "The Hood must have overridden *Thunderbird 5*'s systems using the main computer in the control room. All we need to do is reprogram that computer."

"And maybe The Hood will bring us snacks while we work," Tin-Tin said sarcastically. "There's no way we can get to that computer, Alan."

"I m—m—might have an idea," said Fermat, who was still fumbling with his clothes. "Data and commands from Tracy Island are sent to *Thunderbird 5* via satellite, right? If we reach the island's satellite station we c—c—could—"

"Blow it up!" Alan said, finishing the thought.

"N—no!" Fermat replied, alarmed. "We could h—hack into it through the diagnostics terminal and give control back to *Thunderbird 5*."

"Good thinking," Alan said. "Let's do it!" He strode off away from the jungle.

"Only one problem," Tin-Tin said. "The satellite station is *that* way. We have to go through the jungle." She pointed in the opposite direction from the way Alan had been headed. "It's going to be dangerous."

Alan thrust out one hand. Tin-Tin put her hand

on his, and Fermat did the same. "Just get us there fast," Alan said. "Our folks are in trouble and if The Hood gets off the island in *Thunderbird 2*, no one can stop him."

"Actually," Fermat said, "he's not g—g—going anywhere for now." Out of his pocket he pulled a palm-size electronic gizmo. Some wires hung limply from the back of the gadget.

"That's the guidance processor from *Thunderbird 2*!" Alan said. "It can't take off without it. Fermat, you're a genius! How did you get this?"

"Alan," Fermat replied, grinning, "what you don't know can't hurt you."

"I need to see the boss," Mullion said, stopping outside the door to the control room. Transom stood to one side, guarding the entrance.

"He can't be disturbed," she said. "He's meditating."

Mullion scowled. "Well, snap him out of it. The equipment's ready for inspection."

"It'll have to wait. His abilities take an enormous amount of energy. He needs time to recharge."

"You don't believe all that mystical stuff, do

you?" Mullion asked, reaching for the door.

Transom flashed him a menacing look and he turned and walked away, sulking.

Alan, Tin-Tin, and Fermat pushed their way uphill through the lush jungle toward their destination.

"Is it f—f—f—" Fermat asked, out of breath already.

"Yes, it's far," Tin-Tin replied.

"Fermat," Alan said quietly, "do you think The Hood can read thoughts or control minds or something?"

"Don't be s—silly. Everything can be explained by science."

Alan nodded. "I'm just trying to figure out The Hood's weakness. Everyone has an Achilles' heel."

"M—my Achilles' heel is actually my *heel* right now," Fermat said. "I've got a blister the size of a capacitor. Tin-Tin, c—can we—"

"No stopping," she replied, without even glancing back.

Fermat shrugged. "Don't you think Tin-Tin is b—b—blossoming?" he whispered to Alan.

Alan looked at him like he was crazy. "'Blossoming?' What's that supposed to mean?"

As they climbed, the slope grew steadily steeper. Tin-Tin had no trouble ascending, but Alan and Fermat kept falling farther behind.

"I hate her," Alan whispered to Fermat. He paused and wiped the sweat from his brow. Fermat stopped, too.

"G—gee, I always thought you had a c—-crush on her," Fermat replied.

"What?" Alan said. "You're crazy."

Tin-Tin glanced back at them. "Okay," she said, "take five." Then her eyes widened. "Alan," she said, "don't move!"

"What is it?" Alan asked, freezing in place.

"Androctonus scorpion," Tin-Tin said, barely whispering.

Alan looked left with his eyes and saw a small, black scorpion perched on his shoulder. He swallowed hard and tried not to shake. "Is it dangerous?" he whispered.

"P—p—point zero two five milligrams of its venom is fatal," Fermat told him.

A droplet of poison dripped from the scorpion's upraised stinger onto Alan's shirt.

"Right," Alan said, his jaw barely moving. "So 'dangerous' is, in fact, an understatement."

9

A Bug in the Works

Tin-Tin stood stock-still, staring intently at the deadly arachnid on Alan's shoulder.

Alan and Fermat held their breath.

Tin-Tin's eyes flashed, and the scorpion flew off Alan's shoulder and sailed down the mountainside.

She blinked and staggered woozily.

"Whoa, Tin-Tin!" Alan said. "What was that?"

Tin-Tin's face grew stern. "Let's get going," she said and began climbing again.

Alan shrugged. "Still think everything can be explained by science?" he asked Fermat.

"Not girls," Fermat replied.

A rainstorm blew in, making their progress even more difficult. As they hiked on, wet and miserable, Alan couldn't help wishing that he was home in a nice warm bath.

Lady Penelope Creighton-Ward reached out a painted toe and pressed her intercom button. Bubbles slid down her smooth leg and back into the bath water. "Parker, we have an emergency," she said. "My tea is stone cold."

"Don't worry, milady," came the reply. "I will rectify the situation immediately." A few minutes later, Parker appeared with a silver tea service and poured her a cup.

She piled up the bubbles around herself and took the tea. "Look at this," she said. "I've discovered that one of the rescued oil workers was an imposter." She brought up a picture of Mullion on the viewscreen beside the tub. A picture of Transom appeared next to Mullion. "He and this woman work for a man known as The Hood—real name, Trangh Belagant. Belagant was assumed dead when his diamond mine collapsed in the jungles of Malaysia." The viewscreen now showed a picture of The Hood without his mask.

Lady Penelope sipped her tea as she continued

reading the information on the screen. "Look here
. . . The Thunderbirds rescued over five hundred
mine workers in the collapse, including Belagant's
brother." She tapped the screen with her toe
again and gasped when a new picture came up.

"Milady, that's Mr. Tracy's loyal manservant,
Kyrano!" Parker said.

"Oh, dear," Lady Penelope replied. "Have the
Thunderbirds responded to any disasters today?"

Parker thought a moment. "Typhoon bearing
down on Singapore, volcanic eruption in Jakarta,
a bridge collapse in Buenos Aires—but no sign of
International Rescue."

"Try the emergency signal while I dress," she said.

Parker nodded and left the room.

Soon dressed, coifed, and perfectly made-up,
Lady Penelope met him in the foyer. "No
response, milady," Parker said.

"Cancel my appointments for today, Parker,"
she said. "The Thunderbirds appear to be in a spot
of trouble."

Minutes later, *FAB 1* streaked down the driveway of the Creighton-Ward mansion and soared
into the sky, heading for the Pacific.

The Hood strode through the Thunderbirds'

Tracy Island

Thunderbird 3 soars above the earth.

Fermat and his dad talk shop.

Alan and Fermat do a simulated preflight check in the cockpit of *Thunderbird 1*.

The Hood shows up on Tracy Island.

Tin-Tin, Fermat, and Alan flee from The Hood.

Fermat fixes a transmitter so he, Alan, and Tin-Tin can communicate with the orbiting *Thunderbird 5*.

Alan, Tin-Tin, and Fermat try to launch an old hoversled.

The sled works, but keeping it under control is another story. . . .

Brains finds himself all tied up.

Alan gets thrown into the deep freeze.

FAB 1 arrives at Tracy Island.

Parker and Lady Penelope are ready for business.

The Hood practices intimidation tactics.

Inside *Thunderbird 5*, it's a race against time.
Will Alan be able to save his dad and brothers?

Alan is a Thunderbird at last.

Thunderbirds are *go*!

launch bay, inspecting the incredible array of machinery assembled there. Mullion walked with him.

"We'll be taking this one labeled MOLE to get into the vaults," Mullion said, indicating a huge machine with a massive tapered corkscrew drill on the front of it.

"Subtle as usual, Mullion," The Hood said, though he meant exactly the opposite.

"I didn't realize we'd be getting points for style. We're robbing banks, remember?" Mullion said.

"Don't worry," The Hood said. He gave him a look that caused Mullion to flinch. "You'll get your money."

Transom climbed down out of *Thunderbird 2*'s cockpit and ran over to them. "There's a problem with the guidance processor," she said.

"What's wrong with it?" Mullion said.

"There isn't one," she replied.

"How soon can you build another?" The Hood asked.

"In a week, maybe six days," Transom said.

The Hood closed his eyes a moment and concentrated. A slight smile drew over his wicked face. "Clever, Alan," he whispered. He turned to Mullion. "The children have it."

"No way," Mullion replied. "They're toast. No one could live through something like that."

"I did," The Hood shot back. He leaned close to the big man. "Get them. Take whatever you need, and make sure you return the guidance processor to me."

Alan and Tin-Tin stood below the huge array of satellite dishes perched high on the side of the volcano. They watched as Fermat fiddled with the innards of a large service box attached to the array. Fortunately, the rain had stopped, so they had plenty of light to work in.

"How we doing, Fermat?" Alan asked.

"Don't rush me, Alan," Fermat replied. "This is very d—delicate equipment." As he spoke, an electrical flash lit the inside of the box and a puff of smoke drifted out. "Which is now very b—b— broken," he said, exasperated.

"Can you fix it?" Alan asked.

"Y—y— maybe, but I'll need something to solder with. I could generate the heat needed by focusing the sun's rays through Tin-Tin's necklace, but I still need some metal to repair the connection."

"We're on the side of a mountain," Alan said.

"Where are you going to find some metal to melt?"

Fermat and Tin-Tin looked at each other, then at Alan. It was clear they had the same thing in mind—Alan's retainer.

Ten minutes and much yelping later, Fermat had managed to extract the needed metal from Alan's mouth. "Awa gwonya hill hu," Alan said, holding his aching jaw.

"What did he say," Fermat asked, keeping his eyes on his work.

"I think it was some sort of apology," Tin-Tin said.

Fermat carefully held Tin-Tin's crystal necklace and focused a beam of light to melt the wire onto the broken circuits. "I think that's . . . got it. Yes! You're the man, Fermat!" he said to himself. The screen on the service handset buzzed to life.

"The first step," Fermat continued, "is to establish the connection to *Thunderbird 5*." He fiddled with the electronics, and a picture of the space station's interior appeared on the uplink's diagnostic screen.

The signal wasn't very good, but they could make out Jeff Tracy and Alan's brothers in the dim interior of the craft. All five looked sweaty, dirty, and tired.

"Dad!" Alan said.

"Alan!" Jeff said, relief washing over his grimy face. "Where are you? Are you safe?"

"I'm at the satellite relay station with Fermat and Tin-Tin," Alan responded. "We're going to hack into the computer system to give control of *Thunderbird 5* back to you."

Jeff nodded. "That just might work."

"It'll take a couple of minutes to transfer the data," Fermat said. "Can you ask John to monitor it on your end?"

"I'm on it," John said.

"We're almost there," Fermat said. "Just another minute."

Suddenly, the signal began to break up.

"They're onto us," Fermat said. "We're being j—jammed!"

"Can you finish?" Alan asked.

"I'll try," Fermat replied.

"Alan, what's going on?" Jeff asked. His image was growing fuzzier by the second.

Alan glanced from the screen to Fermat, working frantically on the unit. "Hang in there, Dad. One more minute."

"It's not going to work, Alan," Fermat said. "The signal's too weak for data transmission."

Alan took a deep breath and put on his bravest face. "Dad, they're jamming our signal. Don't worry, though. I'll take care of everything."

"Negative!" Jeff said. "It's too dangerous. Follow emergency procedure. Wait for Lady Penelope at the rendezvous point. Do you read me?"

The picture blurred and Jeff and his sons vanished from the viewscreen.

"Dad!" Alan called. "Dad!"

Tin-Tin put her hand on Alan's shoulder. "I'm sorry," she said. "This is hard on all of us. We all miss our parents."

Alan shook his head. "No. It's okay. I'm fine."

"You don't have to be such a t—tough guy, Alan," Fermat said. "I'm worried sick about my dad."

"Look," Alan said, steeling his jaw, "we have to go. The jamming means The Hood knows we're alive."

"Worse than that," Fermat said, "the transmission will tell him exactly—"

The roar of a powerful engine cut him off.

A fast-moving, four-wheel-drive armored buggy,

with Mullion behind the wheel, raced up the mountainside toward them.

"Alan's right," Tin-Tin said. "We have to go. Follow me." She darted off down the hillside, leading them into the jungle with Mullion in hot pursuit.

10

A Desperate Gamble

Huge wet leaves whipped around the three friends, lashing their bodies as they raced down-hill.

The sounds of Mullion's four-wheeler grew steadily louder. Alan and Fermat panted heavily as they ran, not daring to look back.

"Tin-Tin, can you slow him down?" Alan asked.

"Yeah," she said.

"Then do it. Meet us at the scrap yard on the west slope," Alan said.

Tin-Tin saluted. "Whatever you say, boss." She peeled away from them into the trees.

"Come on, Fermat," Alan said, heading in the opposite direction.

Running as fast as they could, the two boys soon came to the scrapyard—a kind of storage area for Brains' less successful experiments. The scrap pile was located at the head of a dusty gulch. During the rainy season, water ran down the riverbed toward the ocean. Now, though, the narrow gorge was bone dry. Alan began hunting around, throwing aside hunks of metal as he went.

"D—do you mind telling me what you're d—d—doing?" Fermat asked.

"We need to get down the mountain fast, right?" Alan asked. "Well, that old hoversled is around here somewhere."

"It was a piece of j—junk," Fermat sputtered.

"But it was really fast," Alan said. "I'm sure you can fix it. Ah! Here it is!"

He reached into a pile of rusting cast-offs and hauled out a machine the size of a Jet Ski. Despite a sleek metal casing, it looked beat-up and incomplete.

"But there's only r—room for one," Fermat said.

Alan set the hoversled down and walked over to a big half-barrel nearby. "We can tow this behind it like a trailer," Alan said.

"That's going to make this harder to c—control, you know."

"No problem," Alan replied confidently.

Despite Fermat's reservations, they began repairing the broken sled and connecting the passenger car. They'd just managed to fire up the engine when Tin-Tin ran into the clearing.

"Where's Mullion?" Alan asked.

"He drove into a hornets' nest," Tin-Tin said.

"A hornets' n—nest?" Fermat repeated.

Tin-Tin smiled triumphantly. "I helped a little. I hit the nest with a branch and sent it flying right into the cockpit of the beach buggy. But we have to get going. I don't know how long those bugs will hold him."

"Come on, let's get out of here," Alan said.

"On this?" Tin-Tin pointed at the hoversled, arching an eyebrow.

"Unless you've got a better idea," Alan shot back.

"Yeah," she replied. "Let's wait for Lady Penelope, like your dad said."

Alan scowled. "Great plan. Sit and wait to get caught. We have to do something now. Right, Fermat?"

"Actually, I agree with Tin-Tin," Fermat said. "I don't think this craft is s—s—safe."

"You don't think anything is s—s—safe," Alan

replied, wanting to take back the words the moment he said them. Awkward silence filled the scrap yard.

"If we're a team," Fermat said, fighting hard not to stutter, "we should make decisions as a t—team."

"Do you want to vote or do you want to get out of here?" Alan asked. "Because I'm going." He grabbed the hoversled's handlebars and prepared to start it. A moment later, Fermat joined him.

"You can be a real jerk sometimes," Tin-Tin hissed at Alan. She took hold of the sled as well.

They rocked it back and forth a couple of times, building up momentum like a bobsled team. Then, with a final heave, they all ran toward the riverbed. Alan kicked the motorcycle-like starter and climbed on as the vehicle shot forward. Tin-Tin and Fermat piled into the trailer.

"R—remember the control difficulties," Fermat called to Alan.

"No problem," the youngest Tracy replied.

"You mustn't exceed four b—bars of boost, or—"

"I said, *no problem*." Alan gunned the throttle and the rocket-like engine burst to life. The sled rose six inches off the ground and zoomed downhill, kicking up dust. The trailer followed close behind, sparks flying whenever it hit a pro-truding rock.

Alan fought for control of the patched-together skimmer as they hurtled down the riverbed. Tin-Tin and Fermat hung on for dear life. The craft swung wider at every turn, the trailer whipping precariously behind the main sled. Several times, Fermat and Tin-Tin nearly flew out of their seats.

A roaring sound, audible even above the hover-sled's engine, caught their attention. Tin-Tin gasped. "He's coming!"

Mullion's armored four-wheeler hurtled out of the jungle straight at them.

Alan twisted the sled's handlebars and it darted sideways, dipping into a depression in the riverbed. Mullion's buggy soared over them, barely missing the tops of their heads. The vehicle skidded sideways and then dropped into the gorge.

Alan glanced back, over the heads of his friends. Mullion's buggy kicked up huge clouds of dust as he gained on them, drawing closer every moment.

"Hang on," Alan called to Fermat and Tin-Tin. He twisted the throttle up all the way, pushing it well past four bars.

G-forces pulled the skin taut on Alan's face and tried to suck the air from his lungs. The makeshift trailer rattled loudly behind him. He heard Fermat yell, "You're going too fast!"

Alan ignored him and concentrated on the riverbed as it rose into a canyon around them. Two jagged rocks loomed ahead—too narrow for Mullion's four-wheeler to squeeze past. If they could make it through there, Alan knew they'd lose him.

He angled the sled toward the boulders and gunned the engine, then skidded hard around a turn, fighting with all his strength to keep on track. He didn't dare look back, for fear that Mullion might be right on top of them.

With a final burst of speed, he shot through the opening in the jagged rocks. The sled screeched, and metal scraped against rock as it squeezed through the narrow opening. Then they were free, shooting forward and away from their pursuer.

Alan laughed. "See? What did I tell you guys?"

He glanced back over his shoulder, and his heart froze. "No!"

On the other side of the narrow rocks the trailer lay overturned. Tin-Tin and Fermat crawled out from under it, looking dazed and battered. Mullion pulled his armored buggy to a halt beside them.

Tears of frustration welled up in Alan's eyes. He turned away from his captured friends and gunned the hoversled downhill. If he was going to save his family, he would have to do it on his own.

11

The Last Chance

The freezer on Tracy Island was very large, very dark, and very, very cold. *A perfect place*, The Hood thought, *to keep prisoners*.

Despite being chilled, Brains, Kyrano, and Onaha all stood quickly when Mullion thrust Fermat and Tin-Tin inside to join them. "Dad!" blurted Fermat.

"F—Fermat!" Brains said, relieved to see his son alive.

"Are you hurt, Tin-Tin?" Kyrano asked.

"I'm fine," Tin-Tin said.

Mullion lashed them all together with rope and then closed the freezer door, locking them inside.

The streamlined pink limo flew over the surface of the Pacific.

"Approaching Tracy Island, milady," Parker said. "Switching *FAB 1* to aqua mode."

"Very good, Parker," Lady Penelope replied.

Parker threw some switches on the dash, and the flying car dived toward the waves. Its wings retracted, and the nose reshaped itself into the sharp prow of a speedboat. Two large fins slid out from the car's sides, and its jet engine converted to a hydronic impeller. When it splashed down, the vehicle resembled a sleek pink catamaran.

A distinctive wake arced from a sub docked at the island's shore toward *FAB 1*. The object making the waves was submerged, but both Parker and Penelope had seen its like before.

"Pardon me, milady," Parker said, "but it would appear we have a torpedo rapidly approaching on the starboard side."

Lady Penelope put down her glass of champagne. "I suppose we should activate electronic countermeasures."

Parker flicked some switches, and then frowned. "Not possible, milady. It appears to be an all-aspect, wide-spectrum device."

Lady Penelope sighed. "Really . . . what a bother." She took a final sip of champagne. "Parker, abandon ship."

"Very well, milady."

Seconds later, the torpedo struck. The explosion sent spray high into the air and rattled the windows in the International Rescue command center. Seated behind Jeff Tracy's desk, The Hood smiled.

"Somebody roll down the window," Jeff Tracy said. "It's getting stuffy in here."

Thunderbird 5, still locked in a death dance with *Thunderbird 3*, grew steadily hotter as its orbit decayed and it drifted into earth's atmosphere. Friction would soon turn the space station into a gigantic oven, before burning it up completely.

"Reentry into atmosphere in thirty-seven minutes," Virgil said.

"Oxygen's out in thirty," Scott noted, "so we won't feel a thing."

"Stop it," Jeff said. "We're not cooked yet."

"Come on, Dad," Gordon moaned. "The situation's hopeless."

Jeff's tired, sweaty face grew stern. "I don't know what that word means. We've still got time, and we've got people on the ground working for us."

"Alan?" John said incredulously. "He's just a kid."

"But he's a Tracy. He'll think of something," Jeff insisted.

Alan desperately wished he could think of some way to help his family. But he wasn't feeling too confident at the moment. Since escaping Mullion, he'd made his way back to the family compound, but he hadn't figured a way out of the fix he'd gotten them all in.

He crouched on a jungle-covered bluff above the Tracy home, hidden from view but still able to observe the compound below.

Gazing out to sea, he saw something that made his heart soar—a life raft. A *pink* life raft.

"Lady Penelope!" he gasped, then clamped his mouth shut for fear someone might have heard him.

The raft seemed to be the central passenger cabin of *FAB 1*, surrounded by an inflatable pink buoyancy ring. Parker sat in the front of the strange craft, pedaling hard to drive the paddle-wheel mechanism at the back. Lady Penelope sat behind him, wearing a one-piece pink swimsuit and holding a pink parasol to keep the sun off her pale skin. As always, she looked stunning.

Parker and Lady Penelope beached their craft near the Tracy compound and headed up toward the house. Alan dashed downhill through the jungle to meet them.

Lady Penelope picked her way across the sand, being careful where she placed her high-heeled sandals. Parker trailed a few steps behind, keeping lookout for any further signs of trouble.

Penelope frowned. "This doesn't look good, Parker," she said.

"No, milady."

She stopped to examine one of Kyrano's hydrangea bushes. "These flowers are absolutely parched. Kyrano would never let such a thing happen."

"Nor, I venture, would any member of the household fire a torpedo at us," Parker added.

"We'll just have to talk to someone about that," Lady Penelope said. They climbed the stairs toward the wide deck in front of the main entrance.

Mullion stepped out and blocked their way. He folded his arms over his massive chest and leered at them. "I should warn you that I know judo, krav maga, and tae kwon do."

Penelope smiled slightly. "And I know Parker."

Parker sprang forward and punched Mullion solidly in the nose. The big man staggered back, and then fell to his knees. Mullion blinked, trying to clear the stars from his eyes.

As Parker rushed in to finish him off, Transom and The Hood appeared on the deck behind the chauffeur.

"Parker!" Lady Penelope warned.

Parker turned as Transom threw a series of blows at his head and face. Parker deflected Transom's attacks easily, but as he did, Mullion rose and clouted Lady Penelope's manservant in the back of the head. Parker hit the deck like a sack of wet cement.

Lady Penelope sighed. "One tries so hard to sort things out on a conversational level, but sometimes, I suppose, it's just not poss—" Without finishing her thought she executed a series of flips and landed between Parker and his foes. She hooked Mullion's ankle with her parasol handle and yanked him off his feet while simultaneously delivering a vicious side kick to Transom.

The Hood's toothy ally flew backward, crashing hard into a wall. Mullion landed flat on his back, cracking his head on the deck.

Lady Penelope knelt beside Parker. He looked up at her with bleary eyes. "Shall I bring the car around, milady?" he asked.

Lady Penelope's blue eyes flashed with anger. "There, there, Parker. You have a bit of a lie-down." She stood, facing the villains once more. Angry and humiliated, Mullion and Transom rushed her.

Penelope vaulted backward, sprang off the railing, and flew over their heads. She twisted in midair and kicked them both in their backs. The hoodlums sprawled forward, falling hard on their ugly faces.

"Lady Penelope, I presume," The Hood said calmly. "Every castle must have its queen."

"Flattery will get you nowhere," she replied, aiming a series of quick punches at his head.

The Hood moved like a snake, swaying to either side, effortlessly deflecting her blows. He dropped down and swept his leg across her ankles. Lady Penelope fell backward, but instead of landing hard, she turned her momentum into a flip and came up ready to fight again.

"You're a formidable opponent, Lady Penelope," The Hood said. "More than a match for most men."

A slight smile tugged the corners of her mouth. "That's not saying much, is it?"

Parker rose to his feet and charged The Hood from behind. The Hood's eyes flashed and he spun up into the air, out of Parker's reach.

Parker looked up, astonished. The Hood came down on top of him and struck him on the head. Parker slumped to the ground, unconscious.

The Hood landed with a tiger's grace and turned to face Lady Penelope once more. "Stand aside," he said.

"Don't try your parlor tricks on me, you sad little man," Lady Penelope sneered. "You have committed a serious crime trespassing on this island, and in about"—she checked her watch—"four seconds, I'm going to get quite cross with you."

She lunged toward The Hood, but as she did, Mullion grabbed her from behind, threw her to the ground, and quickly tied her up. Transom tied up Parker.

The Hood smiled. Then, without turning around, he said, "So, Alan, how are you?"

In the bushes nearby, a chill ran down Alan's

spine. He'd arrived too late, and now Lady Penelope was in the hands of their enemies.

"I hope you don't think I'm going to chase you," The Hood said, clearly still addressing Alan. Then he turned to Mullion and nodded.

Mullion kicked the back of Parker's head.

"You can make him stop, Alan," The Hood said quietly. "You have something that belongs to me."

Mullion kicked Parker again.

Alan scrambled out of the bushes. "Stop! I'll give it to you."

"Alan, don't!" Lady Penelope said.

Slowly, Alan took the guidance processor from his pocket and held it out to The Hood. Then he cocked his arm and threw it with all his might. The processor sailed into the air.

The Hood's eyes flashed, and the processor arced straight into his hand. He grasped it covetously. "You've made a match of it, Alan, I'll give you that," he said. "Mullion, put them in the freezer with the others."

12

Prisoners of The Hood

Alan, Parker, and Lady Penelope landed hard on the cold floor of the giant freezer. Mullion slammed the door behind them and locked it. It took a moment for the captives to realize that they were not alone.

"Are you okay?" Alan asked Fermat and the other prisoners when he saw them.

"No thanks to you," Tin-Tin shot back.

Alan scowled at her. "To tell the truth, I wasn't talking to you." He turned to Fermat. "So, how does it feel to be right all the time?"

A slight smile tugged at the corners of Fermat's lips. "Not b—bad, actually."

"I'm so sorry, Fermat," Alan said.

"We make quite a pair," Fermat said. "It's hard for me to t—t—talk and hard for you to listen." The friends grinned at each other.

Alan turned to Brains. "How long before Dad and my brothers burn up in the atmosphere?"

"C—calculating *Thunderbird 5*'s descent velocity, um . . ." He grew pensive for a moment, then shook his head. "It's so c—c—cold I can't think."

Fermat slid over to his dad and punched in some numbers on Brains' calculator watch. "You just have to factor in the angle of approach." After a few moments, Fermat sighed grimly. "Three minutes."

"Don't go to sleep!" Jeff Tracy commanded.

His four older sons gazed up at him, their eyes glassy and their breath coming in short gasps. John began to nod off.

Jeff lurched across the compartment and shook him.

"Stay awake!" Jeff said desperately.

John perked up a bit. Jeff went back to rewiring the control panel in the wall, knowing he couldn't finish the job before it was too late. Their orbit was rapidly decaying and their air nearly gone.

If something didn't happen soon, they'd suffo-
cate and then burn up on reentry.

Thunderbird 2 lumbered out of the underground hangar and onto the hidden runway near
the beach. The long line of palm trees on either
side of the strip folded back on cleverly concealed
pivots to let the huge aircraft pass. *Thunderbird 2*
came to a stop at the edge of the airstrip as a
huge blast-shield folded out of the ground
behind it.

The Hood, Mullion, and Transom strapped
themselves into the aircraft's cockpit. The rest of
The Hood's men lay waiting, along with the *Mole*,
in the cargo bay.

"I've installed the guidance processor," Transom
said. "*Thunderbird 2* is ready for takeoff."

"And the sub?" The Hood asked.

"It's returning to base," Mullion replied.

The Hood nodded slowly. "What is our ETA for
London?"

"Under an hour," Mullion replied. "Bank of
England, here we come!"

Thunderbird 2's engines flared to life, belching
huge gusts of smoke and flame. The runway tilted
up in front of them, allowing a short, speedy takeoff.

Transsom pushed the control stick forward and they shot up the ramp, zooming into the sky. Moments later, the villains and their stolen ship disappeared into the clouds.

"We've got to get to the control room to repro-gram the main computer!" Alan said.

"Right," Lady Penelope agreed. "There's been quite enough losing for one day. Parker, I have an idea."

She looked at her high heel, then at a buildup of icicles hanging like stalactites from the ceiling of the freezer.

Guessing her intention, Parker positioned him-self beneath the ice.

Lady Penelope lined up the shot. She kicked her leg high into the air. Her sandal sailed off, smash-ing hard into the ice. One of the icicles broke loose and fell.

Parker held his hands out behind him. The jagged ice sliced neatly through the ropes between Parker's wrists. He picked up the ice and cut Lady Penelope and the rest free.

She smiled. "Come on, Parker," Lady Penelope said. "Let's give the bad guys a good thrashing."

"Yes, milady," Parker replied.

Lady Penelope punched the access code into the keypad on the freezer door.

"Blast!" she said. "They must have reprogrammed the lock at the central computer. Parker, see what you can do with this."

Parker examined the door.

"It seems to be a straightforward six-lever mortise, milady," Parker said.

Penelope smiled. "I love it when your checkered past comes in handy."

Less than a minute later, the freed captives dashed into the main control room. The video screens on the wall showed Jeff, John, Virgil, Scott, and Gordon lying unmoving in the oxygen-deprived space station. Another screen tracked a radar image of *Thunderbird 5* as it neared the point of no return. A clock on the wall counted down the seconds until reentry.

"Less than a minute left!" Alan cried.

Brains and Fermat sprinted to the control panel and began working feverishly. "It I—looks like they slipped a backdoor key into the access codes," Fermat said.

"I'll follow your lead, son," Brains said confidently.

Alan, Lady Penelope, and the rest exchanged

nervous glances as Fermat and Brains typed lines of code into the computers.

"I'm in!" Fermat announced. "I just need someone on the other end to confirm the access protocol."

Brains switched open a communications channel. "Control to *Thunderbird 5*. Come in, Mr. Tracy. Can you hear me?"

Jeff and the others didn't move. Brains' voice echoed eerily around the control room.

"Twenty seconds until reentry!" Fermat said.

"*Thunderbird 5*, come in!" Brains called. He slammed his hand on the control console. "Come on, Jeff! Wake up!"

High above them, Jeff's eyes flickered open. You know, Brains," he said hoarsely, "I think that's the first time you've ever called me by my first name."

He and the boys stumbled to *Thunderbird 5*'s control panels. Just typing seemed to take all their energy.

Alan grabbed the microphone. "Hurry, Dad! Hurry!"

"P—please confirm access protocol," Fermat said, his voice cracking.

John Tracy's weary fingers fumbled across the keyboard. "Confirmed!" he gasped.

"You have control!" Brains said. "B—b—boost *Thunderbird 5* to geostationary orbit immediately!"

Jeff seized the space station's manual control stick and moved it forward. Mighty retro-rockets fired as the screen showing time to reentry counted down: 5 . . . 4 . . . 3 . . . 2 . . . 1. . . .

The video screen in the Tracy Island control room broke up. The picture vanished. Empty static hissed over the airwaves.

"We were too late!" Tin-Tin cried.

But then Jeff's weary voice crackled over the radio. "F.A.B., Brains," he said. "It looks like we're good to go."

A moment later, the video flickered back. The *Thunderbird 5* crew leaned over the ship's controls, dirty and weary, but very much alive. The control room monitors confirmed *Thunderbird 5*'s flight path back into geostationary orbit.

There were cheers all around.

"Dad, are you all right?" Alan asked.

"We're all fine," Jeff replied. "But we've still got work to do. Where's The Hood?"

"He's headed for L—L—London in *Thunderbird 2*, Mr. Tracy," Brains replied. He called up a map in both control rooms showing *Thunderbird 2*

streaking toward England.

"He's got the *Mole* on board!" Alan cried.

"*Thunderbird 3* has lost a booster," John announced. "We'll never get there in time."

Alan moved closer to the video screen. "Let me go after The Hood! He'll destroy everything you've built—everything the Thunderbirds stand for."

"Negative, son," Jeff responded. "It's too dangerous."

"I can do this," Alan said, his eyes burning with determination. "You know I can." Then, as if catching himself, he moved beside Fermat and Tin-Tin. "I mean, *we* can do this."

13

Thunderbirds on the Rampage

For a moment, Jeff Tracy seemed torn between his duties as father and as commander of the Thunderbirds. Finally, he nodded. "We'll meet you there, son. Thunderbirds are *go!*"

Alan, Fermat, and Tin-Tin took up positions in front of the portrait wall. They looked at one another nervously.

"We're really going?" Tin-Tin asked, her voice squeaking slightly.

"Yep," Alan replied.

"Oh, boy," Tin-Tin said breathlessly.

Lady Penelope stepped into place next to them, and Brains moved to the control switch on Jeff's desk.

"Ready, Fermat?" Alan asked.

"N—n—n . . . I guess," Fermat replied.

Brains threw the switch and the wall flipped backward, hurling them down the launch tube leading to *Thunderbird 1*. The youngsters screamed as though on a roller coaster; Lady Penelope smiled.

Inside the mighty rocket, they quickly slipped on International Rescue uniforms and climbed into the cockpit. Alan and Fermat seated themselves at the controls, with Lady Penelope and Tin-Tin taking position in the jump seats behind.

Alan glanced over the long rows of readouts and switches, momentarily overwhelmed. "Right, um . . . set primary fuel pumps."

"Alan," Fermat said, "don't you m—mean the auxiliary booster relays?"

Alan glanced angrily at his friend for a moment, but then he smiled. "You're right, Fermat. I'm glad you're on our team."

They completed the preflight routines and fired up the engines. *Thunderbird 1*'s mighty rockets burst to life as the hangar ceiling rolled away above them.

"Off we go," Lady Penelope said confidently.

She gave Tin-Tin's hand a reassuring squeeze.

Alan and Fermat pushed the accelerator levers forward.

On the island's surface, the Tracy swimming pool rolled sideways into a hidden recess, revealing the huge silo below. An instant later, *Thunderbird 1* shot into the sky, trailing fire and steam. In moments, it broke the sound barrier, shaking the surface of the Pacific Ocean below with a deafening boom.

Alan glanced out the cockpit window at the world speeding past below. On a semi-ballistic trajectory, they'd reach London in no time.

"It I—looks like *Thunderbird 3* is about to initiate separation from *Thunderbird 5*," Fermat said, checking some instruments. "And *Thunderbird 2* is on final approach to London."

"F.A.B., Fermat," Alan said. "I know The Hood's weakness. We can stop him if we get there in time."

"Going to maximum thrust," Fermat replied. He hit a button, and acceleration G-forces slammed all of them back into their seats.

Jeff's voice came over the radio. "*Thunderbird 3* to *Thunderbird 1*," he said, "we're on our way. See you in London."

"F.A.B." Alan replied.

A sonic boom shook the placid surface of the river Thames as *Thunderbird 2* rocketed over London toward Tower Bridge and the banking district beyond. People pointed in amazement as the mighty aircraft zoomed just over the skyline. What rescue mission had brought the Thunderbirds to England this day?

Thunderbird 2 buzzed low under the bridge, its wings barely clearing the span. The machine's wake shattered a thousand windows as it arced past the riverfront.

The aircraft's powerful retros fired as it approached Jubilee Gardens. Pedestrians jammed the block below. Everyone looked up as the titanic green *Thunderbird* approached. Passengers riding the city's monorail craned their necks to see what was going on.

Thunderbird 2 descended like a giant bird of prey, heedless of the people who might be crushed beneath its enormous weight. Tourists scurried out of the way as the huge machine landed. One of *Thunderbird 2*'s struts landed atop an ice cream van, squashing it flat. The van's owner barely scrambled to safety in time.

The crowd squawked angrily, their admiration turning to apprehension. News vans descended on the scene and quickly began filming.

Thunderbird 2 rose up on its stanchions, revealing the equipment pod beneath. The aircraft's exterior speaker hummed to life. "Due to a recent change in management," said the amplified voice of Mullion, "the Thunderbirds no longer rescue . . . we destroy."

At that, the pod's front door dropped open and the *Mole* rolled out. It was larger than a freight train and more heavily armored than a squad of tanks. At its rear were four rocket-like engines, at its front a huge, twisted, screwlike cone. It lumbered forward, crushing a fountain and several abandoned picnic tables as it went.

People ran screaming from the scene. The *Mole* pivoted on its massive treads and began boring into the ground. As the huge machine dug, the earth shook.

Inside the *Mole*'s cockpit, The Hood said, "Set a course for the vault."

The *Mole* turned and headed toward the monorail tracks and Westminster Bridge. It heaved up the earth as it passed, causing nearby buildings to tremble.

"Sir," Transom said, studying a bewildering array of controls, "if we continue on our present course, we'll sever the monorail's subterranean supports. Shall I correct our trajectory?"

"Stay on course," The Hood replied quietly.

"B—but, sir," she said, "we'll cause a major disaster."

The Hood leaned back in his seat. "We won't . . . the Thunderbirds will."

The *Mole* shuddered only slightly as it ground through the monorail's concrete-and-steel support stanchion. Transom glanced nervously at her boss; The Hood merely smiled.

Aboard *Thunderbird 1*, Fermat had tuned in local video broadcasts to help them locate *Thunderbird 2*.

"There seems to be some confusion," Lisa Lowe reported, "about which side the Thunderbirds are on. We're trying to get a reaction from the prime minister about the announcement that came over *Thunderbird 2*'s loudspeaker moments ago. Wait a minute! Oh, this is terrible! The monorail is collapsing!"

Alan and the rest watched in horror as the rail line snapped near the shore of the Thames. Huge pieces of cement crashed into the water. Stanchions buckled, and the rail itself dipped toward the surface of the river. The monorail train that had been crossing the span lurched toward the water. Only a slim connecting cable kept one monorail car from sliding into the deep.

"Do you see that, Dad?" Alan asked.

"F.A.B.," Jeff responded. "Do what you can. We'll be there soon."

Lady Penelope glanced at Alan and Fermat, her voice tight and controlled. "Get us down, boys!"

Alan angled the ship to land next to *Thunderbird 2.*

"Alan, we're going too fast," Fermat said.

"We have no choice," Alan responded. "Hang on!" He flicked some switches and kicked on the retros. Warning alarms blared in the cockpit. Alan and Fermat fought hard to keep the aircraft stable.

With a bone-shaking thud they landed.

"Textbook, boys," Lady Penelope said.

Alan turned on the outside loudspeaker and took the microphone. "Attention, citizens," he said, putting on his most grown-up voice. "The situation is under control." His voice cracked on the last word.

Alan, Fermat, Tin-Tin, and Penelope shut down the flight systems, unstrapped themselves, and prepared to leave the ship.

"That cable won't hold much longer," Lady Penelope said.

"We need *Thunderbird 2*!" Alan said, dashing for the exit.

"F.A.B.," replied Tin-Tin and Fermat, following right behind.

They sprinted to *Thunderbird 2*, pausing only long enough to deactivate the big aircraft's anti-intruder systems.

"Thank g—goodness The Hood didn't have time to scramble the codes," Fermat said.

They raced to the cockpit and fired up the systems. Alan glanced at the tracking screen, which showed the *Mole* nearly on top of its target. "The Hood!" Alan cried. "He's getting away!"

Tin-Tin glanced at one of the viewscreens monitoring the news broadcasts. "Those people can't hold out much longer," she said.

"What do you want to do, Alan?" Fermat asked.

Alan took a deep breath. "We're the Thunderbirds. Our duty is to save those people." He fired up the VTOL engines and *Thunderbird 2* lifted lightly into the air. They raced to the monorail car hanging just above the water.

"Okay, Fermat," Alan said, "I'm going to need you to fire a grappling rocket at that support beam."

"B—b—but I've n—n—never d—d . . . I don't think I can . . ."

Alan looked confidently at his friend. "Real bravery is being scared and doing the right thing anyway. The Thunderbirds need you right now. Those people need you. *I* need you."

"F.A.B—B—B., Alan," Fermat said, pressing a button. A flap on *Thunderbird 2*'s underbelly opened, revealing a row of missiles. Fermat took a deep breath and lined up the shot using the cockpit's targeting control system. He fired.

The grappling missile zoomed out, trailing a cable behind it. The grapple locked onto the tracks, and *Thunderbird 2* reeled in the slack.

"Okay, slowly now," Alan said, more to himself than the others.

He eased back the stick and pushed up on the thrusters. Slowly but surely, *Thunderbird 2* rose into the air, and the line began to pull the rail straight once more.

"We're doing it!" Tin-Tin exclaimed.

But the cracks in the monorail track were

growing larger by the second.

"If it'll just hold a m—m—minute longer!" Fermat said.

With a horrifying snap, the monorail track split in two.

Alan, Fermat, and Tin-Tin watched helplessly as the train carriage rolled down the broken rail and plunged into the deep water below.

14

More Than All the Money . . .

The cavernous steel vault stretched more than three stories high. Thousands of security boxes lined its towering walls. Catwalks circled the levels connecting the main storage areas and side passages with the maintenance and security tunnels surrounding the complex. Ten-foot-thick concrete walls reinforced with steel protected the depository walls; its door was made of a virtually impregnable titanium alloy. Only a fool or a madman would attempt to rob the Bank of England.

The whole vault shook as the *Mole* bored in from beneath. The big corkscrew drill bit filled the air with clouds of dust and shards of concrete and steel. The mighty machine ground to a halt and its top hatch opened. The Hood, Mullion, and Transom stepped out. Satisfied smiles spread across their wicked faces.

Using a punch gun, the three began to rip open the safety deposit boxes and loot the place.

Monitoring the *Mole*'s progress from the cockpit of *Thunderbird 1*, Lady Penelope decided to take action. She ran from Jubilee Gardens and hailed a cab to take her to the bank.

Fermat cut loose the useless tow cable before the falling rail could drag *Thunderbird 2* into the water.

"I'm going down in *Thunderbird 4*," Alan said. "Bring us low, over the river."

"F.A.B.," Fermat responded.

Alan hurried down into the equipment pod. Tin-Tin followed after him.

"Stay in the launch bay," he told her. "We may need someone near the winches."

Tin-Tin nodded as Alan climbed into *Thunderbird 4*, a compact, high-tech submarine. As Fermat swung low over the water, Alan opened the pod bay door, and *Thunderbird 4* splashed into the murky Thames.

Alan switched on the sub's exterior lights and headed straight for the monorail track. "Okay," he said, "I'm going to deploy the fusion probe and cut through the bolts holding the car to that broken piece of rail. I need you to get a line on the compartment to pull it free."

In the cockpit of *Thunderbird 2*, Fermat stared at the targeting screen. "I can't get a fix on it," he said. "The water's too murky—I might puncture the passenger compartment."

Tin-Tin's voice came over the radio from the cargo bay intercom. "They have only a few minutes of air at most," she said. "I'll attach the line manually. Get as close to the water as you can, so I can dive in."

"B—b—but it's too risky," Fermat said.

"It's either that or let them all drown," she replied.

Fermat adjusted the hover jets and brought *Thunderbird 2* down just above the tops of the waves. Tin-Tin dived out of the launch bay, towing an unbreakable mesh line with her.

In *Thunderbird 4*, Alan circled the submerged train compartment and cut the restraining bolts as he went. His lights playing across the windows of the train revealed the faces of the frightened people trapped inside. The car was rapidly filling with water; the passengers had only a few minutes left.

Tin-Tin swam toward the trapped carriage, fighting the currents and the backwash from *Thunderbird 4*'s engines. Unconcerned about her own safety, she carefully attached the towline to the flooding car.

Her breath was nearly gone. The chilly water made her limbs feel like lead. She looked toward the surface, seemingly miles above. She knew she wouldn't make it. She felt dizzy. She needed to breathe, but the surface was so far away. . . .

Suddenly, *Thunderbird 4* plunged into view. Alan positioned the sub above her and opened the airlock. Tin-Tin swam in, exhaling the last of her air as the water receded around her. She opened the inner door and joined Alan in the cabin.

"Good timing," she gasped.

He smiled at her and nodded. "What took you so long?" He cut the last of the bolts holding the carriage to the rail, then radioed Fermat. "All clear! Fermat, these people need a lift."

"F.A.B., Alan! Commencing reverse thrust!"

Thunderbird 2 climbed slowly into the sky, taking the drenched passenger compartment with it.

In moments, the monorail train cleared the water. Fermat lowered it safely to the banks of the Thames. Fire and rescue personnel swept forward and quickly freed the soggy passengers.

Alan beached *Thunderbird 4* while Fermat landed *Thunderbird 2* nearby. Switching on the crafts' anti-intruder devices, they ran to greet each other.

"We did it!" Alan said, giving first Fermat and then Tin-Tin a hug. He and Tin-Tin stared at each other a moment. Then they both blushed and turned away.

The roar of rocket engines sounded overhead. They all looked up as *Thunderbird 3* landed atop the embankment just a few yards away. Alan and the others raced up the steps to greet the returning astronauts.

Gordon, Scott, John, Virgil, and Jeff raced forward and smothered the kids with big hugs.

"Glad you could finally join us, Dad," Alan said.

Jeff Tracy smiled at his youngest boy. "Don't get cocky after just one mission." He turned to the rest of his sons. "We've still got a dangerous situation here. I need you boys to close down the accident scene, help the authorities, and keep the Thunderbirds secure."

"Okay," Scott said to the rest, "let's clean it up!" He and his brothers sprang to action.

"Dad," Alan said, "Lady Penelope went after The Hood."

"She may need our help then," Jeff responded. "We'll take *Thunderbird 1*." He, Alan, Fermat, and Tin-Tin sprinted toward the mighty rocket.

As they approached, the entry hatch slid open and Parker peered out. "Might you be in need of a lift?" he asked.

"Parker, how'd you get here?" Alan asked, please to see their friend.

"Hitched a ride by using one of Professor Hackenbacker's experimental single-use shuttles," Parker replied.

"It's good to have you with us," Jeff said as they all climbed aboard and settled into their seats. The head of the Tracy family took the controls and blasted off toward the bank.

"Dad . . . ?" Alan said as they flew.

"Yes, son?"

"That stuff The Hood said, about your leaving him to die . . . He was lying, right?"

Jeff Tracy shook his head. "No. It's not as simple as that, Alan. The Hood kept his mine workers in chains. They couldn't even run when the tunnels collapsed. We had to seal the shaft or hundreds more would have died. So I made a choice." He sighed. "You can't save everyone, Alan. It doesn't matter how hard you try or how brave you are. It doesn't matter if they're good or bad. It doesn't even matter if it's someone you love—or that you'd give up your life in a second to save hers. You just can't save everyone." He looked into Alan's eyes and a moment of unbearable sadness passed between them.

"I miss Mom," Alan said finally.

"Me too, son."

The Hood pulled a velvet bag out of a broken safe and poured the contents into his hands. Diamonds spilled through his fingers like glittering droplets of water and fell to the floor. Oddly, the loot didn't even seem to satisfy him. "Ashes to ashes . . . diamonds to diamonds," he muttered.

He stood and brushed off his hands. Then, without turning around, he said, "Lady Penelope. What an unpleasant surprise."

Penelope stood near the vault's main door, holding a gun on him. "Don't be rude," she said calmly. "Now, just back into the corner, and don't move."

The Hood waved his hand, and the gun flew out of her grasp. "Mullion!" the villain called.

Before Lady Penelope could react, Mullion leaped forward and pinned her arms to her sides. She twisted and tried to worm out of his grasp, but her agility was no match for his strength.

"Oh, that's not cricket," she said, exasperated.

"I'm sorry," The Hood replied. "The only part of that sport I liked was winning."

15

Thunderbirds to the Rescue

Mullion snapped shut the handcuffs, chaining Lady Penelope into one of the cages on the lowest level of the bank's main vault. The transport cages, partially filled with gold bars and other loot, sat next to the *Mole*. The mighty digging machine's huge drill-like nose jutted up from the vault's floor. The *Mole*'s hatches lay open, ready to winch the loaded cages aboard once Mullion had finished filling them.

Transom smiled as Lady Penelope struggled against the chains, trying to free herself. It was no use.

Mullion laughed cruelly.

The Hood nodded, pleased. Then he paused. "The Thunderbirds," he said. "They're here."

Mullion had learned to trust his master's instincts. He and Transom sprinted toward the vault's main entrance.

"Be sure to kill them all," The Hood called after his cronies.

Jeff, Alan, and the rest dashed through the vault's main door.

"Parker," Jeff said, "keep an eye on the kids while I find The Hood."

"Very good, Mr. Tracy," Parker replied.

Jeff sprinted around a corner and out of sight. Alan glanced from his father to his friends. "Look out, Parker!" he cried.

Parker whirled, expecting a new menace, but it was only a ploy by Alan. As soon as the chauffeur turned, the youngest Tracy ran off after his father.

"Master Tracy! Stop!" Parker called.

"Parker, I—look out!" said Fermat.

Parker rounded on him, annoyed. "That's enough of that," he began. Then he spotted Mullion stepping around a nearby corner.

"Don't move!" Mullion ordered.

Parker, Tin-Tin, and Fermat turned to go the

other way, but Transom jumped from an alcove and blocked their exit. The Hood's toothy minion planted her feet in a challenging stance, balled up her fists, and glared at them.

"W—what are you waiting for, Parker?" Fermat asked, glancing nervously from one villain to the other.

"I can't hit a lady," Parker replied.

"Allow me," Tin-Tin said. She hurled herself forward, dropping to the polished marble floor and sliding between Transom's legs. Before the lady scientist could react, Tin-Tin kicked her rear end.

Transom staggered into a wall. Tin-Tin rose and sprinted off down the corridor. Red-faced with anger, Transom ran after her.

Before Parker and Fermat could retreat, Mullion cut them off. "I've been waiting to get my hands on these little brats," he said menacingly.

Parker smiled and cracked his knuckles. "And I've been waiting to get my hands on *you*." He stepped between Fermat and Mullion and raised his fists.

Mullion surged forward and punched Parker in the face.

The chauffeur blinked and smiled. "Not bad," he said. "Try this." He counterpunched to Mullion's gut and the big man staggered back.

"Pretty good," Mullion replied. "Let's have another go."

Jeff dashed onto the lowest level of the main vault. Catwalks snaked overhead, casting eerie shadows throughout the chamber. The *Mole*, nearly ready to depart, stuck up out of the floor in the center of the huge room. Its metallic bulk towered into the air. The main hatch reached up to the level of the first catwalk. Big cages, piled with loot, stood on either side of the drilling machine. Lady Penelope rattled the bars of her cage as she spotted the Thunderbirds' leader.

"Penny!" Jeff called, racing toward her.

"Jeff, watch out!" she cried.

Jeff turned as The Hood stepped from the shadows.

"Did you save them *all* this time, Jeff?" The Hood purred. "Or did you leave someone behind?"

"I didn't make you what you are," Jeff shot back.

"It's not *me* you have to convince," The Hood

said. He turned toward the vault door as Alan skidded in.

"Leave my son out of this," Jeff said, lunging toward The Hood.

The Hood stretched out his hand and his eyes flashed.

Jeff flew off the floor and sailed thirty feet through the air. He crashed hard into the cage beside the *Mole*, landing at Lady Penelope's feet. Before he could get up, the cage door slammed shut and locked.

"Dad!" Alan cried.

The Hood, his eyes gleaming, his head glistening with sweat, walked slowly toward Alan. "I'm disappointed, Alan. I thought we were kindred spirits."

"Well, we're not. You're a creep. And I'm Jeff Tracy's son."

"You certainly are," The Hood replied. He waved his hand. Alan flew through the air and slammed into a wall.

Alan's breath rushed out as he slumped to the floor. He looked up just as a piece of the ceiling fell toward him.

Tin-Tin ran through the vault's winding corridors

with Transom close behind. Ahead of them, the corridor stopped abruptly in a dead-end vault. Transom smiled, showing her bad dental work. She had Tin-Tin trapped. Tin-Tin glanced from the vault to some pipes running overhead.

Transom lunged forward. "Gotcha!"

Tin-Tin leaped up out of Transom's reach and grabbed one of the pipes. She turned her jump into a swing, flying up over the conduit like a gymnast circling a high bar. Transom passed harmlessly beneath her and stumbled into the wall of the dead end vault.

Tin-Tin landed lightly on her feet behind Transom.

As Transom whirled, Tin-Tin slammed the vault door shut, locking Transom inside.

Tin-Tin did a mock curtsy and dashed off to find her friends.

Parker and Mullion stood a few feet apart, gazing wearily into each other's eyes. They'd exchanged blows for long minutes, each refusing to surrender or give any ground.

Lady Penelope's chauffeur rubbed his gut. "Now, that's a punch!" he said appreciatively to Mullion.

Fermat leaned forward and whispered to Parker, "Can we hur—hur— wrap this up?"

Parker panted wearily, not taking his eyes off Mullion. "What do you have in mind, Master Hackenbacker?"

"Strategically speaking," Fermat replied, "the b—best odds of success lie with the Parker Punch."

"I concur," Parker said, blinking the sweat from his eyes.

Mullion, battered and bruised, aimed an exhausted blow at Parker's head.

Parker ducked out of the way and wound up his punch.

As Mullion lurched forward, Parker smashed a solid right uppercut to his chin.

Mullion's head snapped back, and he fell to the floor, unconscious.

Fermat and Parker smiled at each other, and then took off to help the others.

Alan spun out of the way as the piece of ceiling crashed to the vault floor beside him. He rose, eyeing the master criminal. The Hood's breath came in short, labored gasps.

Alan charged forward, but The Hood flipped up

over his head. Alan crashed into a pillar where The Hood had been and fell to the floor, dazed. The Hood soared through the air and landed shakily on the catwalk above.

"You want so desperately to walk in daddy's footsteps," he hissed.

With an effort, The Hood gestured and Alan rose off the ground, as though someone had grabbed him by the neck. Choking, Alan kicked at the empty air.

The Hood leaned on the catwalk railing, his eyes blazing. "Did you really think you could challenge me?"

With another gesture, he dropped Alan to the floor. The Hood stumbled but managed to catch himself. Alan nearly landed on some sparking electrical wires, but he rolled out of the way just in time.

"Alan, just run!" Jeff Tracy called to his son.

"He's getting weaker," Alan called back. "He can't last much longer."

"Neither can you!" Jeff replied.

The Hood walked across the catwalk toward the *Mole*'s upper hatch.

Desperate, Alan began to climb the outside of the huge machine. He pushed past the *Mole*'s grinding teeth and scrambled up onto the big drill.

The Hood noticed. His eyes flashed, very weakly this time. A switch inside the *Mole*'s cockpit activated and the machine's big gears began to move.

The spiral of the drill lurched, and Alan held on for dear life. Below him, the grinding teeth whirled to life. As the drill bit built up speed, Alan swung onto it and launched himself into the air.

He grabbed for the catwalk but caught hold with only one hand.

The Hood turned and walked back toward him.

"Alan!" Jeff Tracy cried. He and Penelope rattled the bars of their cage, but they were locked in tight.

The Hood smiled at the leader of the Thunderbirds. "I'm so glad you could be here to see this, Jeff," he said. He raised one foot above Alan's hand. "Good-bye, Alan."

Alan glanced from The Hood to the grinding machinery below. If he let go, the *Mole* would crush him.

At that moment, Tin-Tin dashed into the room. She spotted Alan dangling from the catwalk and screamed, "Nooo!"

Alan looked at her; their eyes met.

Tin-Tin reached out with her hands, and waves of force shook the room. The catwalk lurched, flipping Alan forward onto it.

The Hood reeled backward from the shock of Tin-Tin's attack. He fell against the metal banister and toppled over. At the last second, he grabbed hold of the railing with one hand.

Alan staggered to his feet.

The Hood dangled precariously, inches away from the *Mole*'s stone-crushing machinery—facing the very fate he had meant for Alan.

Alan gazed coldly at him. The Hood swayed below him, helpless. With each moment, the criminal's grip slackened a little bit more.

Fermat and Parker appeared in a doorway on the vault's bottom level. They gazed up at Alan, along with Jeff, Penelope, and Tin-Tin, watching The Hood slip toward his doom. All of them held their breath.

"Leave me, Alan," The Hood sneered. "Leave me to die—like your father did!" He let his fingers slide from the rail.

Alan's hand shot out and grabbed The Hood's wrist.

"I don't want to save your life," Alan said, "but that's what we do."

Slowly, with every muscle in his body aching, Alan pulled The Hood to safety.

The British police and Scotland Yard arrived quickly. International Rescue gladly turned The Hood, Transom, and Mullion over to the authorities. As the police led The Hood toward the squad car, the heavily bound criminal lunged toward the Tracy family.

"See you soon," he said, smiling wickedly.

The police pushed him into the waiting car. Jeff and Lady Penelope joined Alan, Fermat, Tin-Tin, and Parker beside *Thunderbird 1*. Suddenly, *Thunderbirds 2* and *3* roared overhead. They did a celebratory barrel roll before shooting off into the sky.

Parker shook his head. "That's definitely showing off."

Jeff put his arm around Alan. "Son, you did a great job today," he said. "I'm proud of you."

"Thanks, Dad," Alan replied, beaming. "Can I drive home?"

Jeff smiled back. "Not a chance."

Epilogue

The golden sun set into the Pacific Ocean, splashing glittering rays across Tracy Island. Most of the island's inhabitants had gathered at the pool. Parker worked on the beach nearby, studiously polishing the rebuilt *FAB 1*.

Jeff flipped burgers on the grill and chatted casually with Lady Penelope. Kyrano and Onaha lounged on the patio, taking some time to relax. John, Virgil, Gordon, and Scott played full-contact water polo in the pool's deep end.

Alan sat at the pool's edge, giving Fermat swimming lessons. Fermat splashed around in the shallow end, wearing a nose clip, water wings, and prescription diving goggles. Brains, dressed in his lab coat as usual, came out of the house to watch. Alan gave him the thumbs-up.

Brains nodded at Alan and beamed proudly at his son.

Tin-Tin came up behind Alan and asked, "So, what do you think?"

"He's getting there," Alan said, still watching Fermat. "After all, he's learning from the best." Then he turned and noticed her.

Tin-Tin looked stunning in her Polynesian silk dress. She'd styled her hair and make-up to resemble one of Lady Penelope's magazine cover shots.

Alan's mouth dropped open. "Tin-Tin," he said, "you look . . ."

"You'd better not make fun of me, Alan Tracy!" she warned.

"No," Alan insisted, "you're really . . . blossoming."

"Eww!" cried Tin-Tin. "Did you just say 'blossoming'?"

Jeff clanged the dinner bell, mercifully saving Alan from further conversation. The boys all clambered out of the pool and stood by the grill. Parker even put down his chamois and joined the rest.

"Tonight is a very special night," Jeff announced. "There were moments when I didn't think any of us would see it. But we're here

tonight because of three incredibly special people."
He glanced at Tin-Tin, Fermat, and Alan.

"The world needs the Thunderbirds," Jeff continued, "and the Thunderbirds need you." He pulled three golden Thunderbirds wing emblems from his pocket and pinned them on. "Congratulations, you've earned it."

The three friends looked down at the glittering pins, then beamed at one another. Alan's older brothers gathered around them, whooping and slapping the newest Thunderbirds' backs.

"Does this mean you won't need *my* help anymore?" Lady Penelope asked Jeff playfully.

Jeff gazed into her eyes. "I'll always need you, Penny." He put his arm around her and smiled. Nearby, a phone rang.

Jeff sighed, pulled a red cellular phone from his pocket, and answered it. "Yes, Madam President?" he said.

Moments later they all dashed into the control center. Virgil, Scott, John, and Gordon took up their positions along the walls, each standing beneath his own portrait. Alan got in line next to them, under his own brand-new portrait.

Fermat and Tin-Tin stood beside Brains, Penelope, and Jeff at the International Rescue command console.

Alan took a deep breath and caught his father's eye. Jeff Tracy grinned and said, "Thunderbirds are *go!*"

The portrait wall flipped backward, sending Alan and his brothers into the Thunderbirds, and off on their next adventure.